For Kristen—
Sins loud,
Sins proud!.
GRL 2014

the trust

Shira Anthony
Venona Keyes

Shira Anthony

Dreamspinner Press

Published by
Dreamspinner Press
382 NE 191st Street #88329
Miami, FL 33179-3899, USA
http://www.dreamspinnerpress.com/

The Trust
Copyright © 2012 by Shira Anthony and Venona Keyes

Cover Art by Catt Ford

ISBN: 978-1-61372-554-2

Printed in the United States of America
First Edition
June 2012

eBook edition available
eBook ISBN: 978-1-61372-555-9

To Bob, the sexiest man who ever sailed the Carolina coast. I look forward to the next twenty years of adventure at your side, wherever that may lead us.

—Shira

To beautiful men of adventure everywhere—especially FVK, wherever he may be. And to my wonderful friend, co-writer, and co-conspirator, Shira.

—Venona

chapter one

The Hitman is Hit

I'm falling down a spiral, destination unknown,
I can't get no connection, can't get through, where are you…
—"Twilight Zone" by Golden Earring

SHIT. Shit, shit, shit!

Blood gushed from his leg, and for just an instant, he watched it with growing anger. Watched it, that was, until the adrenaline kick-started his brain and he realized he would die if he kept bleeding like this.

Gotta stop the bleeding, he thought with desperation.

He dragged himself to the women's bathroom, pushed hard on the door, and stumbled in. Between the sound of the door slamming against the wall and the sight of all the blood, the startled women inside screamed and ran out.

Blood coated everything he touched. He leaned against a stall door, and it swung open under his weight. One hand applying pressure to the gunshot wound, he elbowed the toilet-paper holder. He fell to the floor and the roll sprang free. He placed the cheap one-ply paper over the wound and pressed down hard—it only took a minute before the roll was a deep crimson.

He tapped the microphone on his chest and shouted, "Agent down! I need an extraction, now!"

"Who's down?" came the calm, even voice in his earpiece.

"I am. Sandoval fucking ambushed me. Caught me in the leg. Hit an artery."

"Anders, where are you?"

"I—" He broke off, looking up to see a slender man leaning casually against the stall door, grinning at him. The Silver Fox, Jason Sandoval. Sandoval wasn't Jake's target, but it seemed as though Jake was *his*. Jake had always detested Sandoval. Now he knew why.

"So… *there* you are. Thanks for leaving me a trail of bloody breadcrumbs to follow."

"Agent Anders, where are you?" the voice in his ear persisted. He ignored it.

"Looks like ya got a bleeder there, Anders."

They had never been friends, but they had been colleagues. Now, Jake wanted nothing more than to blow the smirk off the other man's face.

Fucking traitor.

"I've had worse," Jake lied. If Sandoval wanted him dead, he'd probably only have to wait a few minutes for him to bleed out. But that wasn't Sandoval's style—he had never been a patient man, and Jake knew it.

"Not sure that's true, but I admire your bravado."

Again, the voice in his ear. "Agent Anders, who's there with you?"

"What do you want, Sandoval?" Jake asked. He'd pretty much always suspected Jason Sandoval was insane. Now he was sure of it.

Who the hell is he working for? Foreign government? Private concern?

They had come here as a team, their mission to intercept a scientist who was in town for a conference. But things had gone horribly wrong. It had been a setup, the entire scenario. Three of their own agents had turned their guns against him and his backup team. But why?

Fucking traitors. All of them.

"Well, I *could* watch you bleed to death. Or I suppose I could just end it for you now. Seems a shame, though. You really were a first-class ops guy, Jake. Now your life is fading away, and I get to witness it."

Jake slowly reached inside his pants.

"Now, now, Jake," drawled Sandoval, "no cheatin'. Take that hand out of your pocket."

"I'm trying to stem the bleeding at the pressure point."

"Like hell."

Jake withdrew his hand and flicked his wrist faster than the other man could follow, impaling him in the right eye with a knife. Sandoval staggered backward and out of the stall without uttering a word. Jake reached for his gun, but it was missing. When had he lost it? He needed to finish Sandoval off before *he* was the one lying on the floor with his brains blown out.

He heard the distinctive muffled "pflnk" of a silencer. With the last scrap of his energy, Jake pushed the stall door open in time to see Sandoval fall backward, hitting the tile wall and sliding onto the floor. He was dead.

"Jake," came a familiar baritone voice. "Reduce your heart rate, just as I taught you. It will slow the bleeding."

Jake closed his eyes. In spite of the ice that flowed through his veins and the drowsiness that threatened to pull him under, he forced himself to meditate. He envisioned the frantic beating of his heart slowing down, imagined the damaged artery closing, the blood clotting, and the wound beginning to heal. The thundering rush of blood in his ears began to ebb. The dizziness subsided. He slowed his breathing, and his heart steadied.

"Good work, Jake," he heard the soothing voice say. "It isn't your time to be with me. Not yet."

"Agent Anders! Agent Anders!" He wanted to swat the earpiece away, but he didn't have the strength.

He blinked, trying to focus his uncooperative eyes on the figure that stood before him. "Trace?" he whispered as he passed out.

"FUCKING traitor Sandoval," Ryan Roberts growled from nearby.

"If Jake hadn't killed him, I'd've gladly done it myself." John Carson—Jake recognized the voice.

"He's a damn lucky bastard." Ryan's voice again.

"Un-fucking-believable. Got that tourniquet on and still had the presence of mind to write the time on his leg," added Carson.

"I gotta hand it to 'im—got Sandoval once in the eye, then turned around and shot 'im to make sure he was dead—all while he's fuckin' bleeding to death."

"Gentleman, Agent Anders needs to rest." A woman's voice this time: soothing, no-nonsense, and familiar.

"Sorry, Dr. Carroll." Carson sounded embarrassed, but Jake could hear the note of concern in his gruff voice. "We just wanted to be here when Jake wakes up."

"He will regain consciousness when his body's ready. He's lost a lot of blood, and he's been in surgery."

"We'll wait," Ryan replied. Jake almost smiled to hear the stubbornness in Ryan's voice.

"Agent Roberts, Agent Carson, the director has called a meeting, and you both need to be in attendance." Stephanie Carroll's voice was now commanding.

Jake felt a strong hand squeeze his shoulder. "You better get your lazy ass outta here, Anders, or I'm gonna have to beat the crap outta ya." The sounds of chairs scraping the floor and fading footsteps followed Ryan's words.

"It's all right, Agent Anders. They're gone," Jake heard a few minutes later.

The dim light of the room was too bright. Jake squinted, blinked several times, and slowly opened his eyes. He had a splitting headache.

"Welcome back to the world of the living, Jake."

Jake attempted to smile back at the gentle-voiced doctor, but it came out more like a grimace.

"Are you in pain?"

"My head feels like it's gonna explode."

"I'll give you something."

Jake watched as the tiny woman took a syringe and injected it into the IV in his arm. He felt warmth radiate from the site of the line as his muscles relaxed and the pounding in his head began to lessen.

"Thanks. I think I feel less 'vincible' now," he said, managing a lopsided grin.

She smiled at him. "Jake, I really can't tell you how impressed I am with the skills you exhibited under the extreme pressure of the situation."

"I had help."

"Oh?"

"The Trace Sim. He told me to slow down my breathing and meditate. I imagined my artery knitting itself back together."

"Impressive. I didn't think the simulation microchips were so detailed in their programming."

Jake shrugged. "Neither did I. It's like he was right there in front of me."

"When our bodies are under acute stress, we often imagine things," she replied in a kind but patronizing tone.

Jake guessed that she'd heard the recording of his call for help and had wondered why he'd spoken Trace Michelson's name.

"He seemed so *real*. Not like the usual Sim."

Her answer was what he'd expected and hoped for: reassuring and kind. "The brain is an amazing organ. In times of severe stress, it can be a powerful tool to ensure survival."

The tension in his shoulders abated with her words.

She's right. It was probably a combination of the Sim and my own imagination. Either way, it worked, right?

She offered him a sympathetic smile. "You need to rest." She checked the IV and made a notation on the chart at the foot of his bed.

She turned to leave, then paused as if considering something. "You know, Jake," she said with a contemplative hand to her chin, "applying a tourniquet made from the toilet roll spindle and your torn shirt was quite remarkable, given the extent of your injury. But you didn't really need it—the artery had already begun to heal on its own. It appears Dr. Michelson's techniques are more effective than we originally thought. Quite fascinating."

"Tourniquet?" It was the second time someone had mentioned it since he'd regained consciousness. But he didn't remember a tourniquet, let alone applying one to himself in the heat of the moment.

"The one you placed on your leg before you lost consciousness."

"I don't remember that. The last thing I remember is Trace."

"Writing the time you placed the tourniquet on your leg required true presence of mind, Jake," she continued, undaunted. "We were able to quickly ascertain how long the circulation had been compromised."

"I don't remember that either." He frowned.

She gave him another reassuring smile. "You really *must* get some rest now. I'll be back to check on you later. Would you like something to drink?"

"Something more than ice chips?" he asked with a hopeful expression.

"I'll see that you get some water."

"Thanks." He closed his eyes. He heard her walk out of the room and close the door behind her.

Tourniquet? Writing the time on my leg? And who killed Sandoval? I couldn't have shot him; I didn't have my gun....

It made no sense. An image of the man with dark hair and slate-blue eyes filled Jake's mind. He'd seen that face many times while training with his Sim. He had known the real man himself years before—Trace Michelson had recruited Jake into the Trust. But for years, it had been only a virtual Trace who had inhabited his mind, training him, sharing his knowledge with his host as all Sims did.

This was different. He was so… real.

He forced his eyes open again and stared up at the ceiling. The gray acoustic tiles provided him with no answers.

"Idiot," he muttered as he fought the overwhelming urge to sleep. "Of course he wasn't there. He's been dead for nearly five years."

chapter two

The Calling Card

No one can ever gain strength by brooding over his weakness.

—Paramananda

VOICES wove in and out of his consciousness, their conversation disjointed.

"…but no one came in or out of that bathroom except a group of women, right after Jake went in."

"…found him with his gun by his side… no other prints but his."

"The bullet we extracted from Sandoval's body was from Jake's gun."

"Gentlemen, you really must let him rest."

Then, at last, silence.

"JAKE."

Through the dim haze of the drugs, he answered the voice that spoke in his mind. *Trace?*

"They mustn't learn the truth of my programming. Not yet."

You are *real!*

"*I am only 'real' in your mind,*" replied the Sim.

No. I'm having a conversation with you. You can't have a conversation with a Sim.

"*What do you believe?*" Jake could almost imagine the sardonic lift of an eyebrow.

I... I saw you. In Union Station. You spoke to me. You saved my life.

"*I did only what a Sim would do. What I was programmed to do. I gave you the benefit of my knowledge. I lent you my experience, that's all.*"

That's bullshit, and you know it. You're a prototype. One of a kind.

"*My programming is more sophisticated than the others', but my function is the same.*"

Jake didn't answer.

"*You will understand it someday,*" said the Sim.

Jake ignored this. *What did you mean when you said that it wasn't my time to be with you?*

"*You will understand,*" the Sim repeated. "*Rest now and heal. And, Jake... trust no one.*"

Nine years before

JAKE leaned on one knee, panting, head bowed, his lip bloodied. Three neighborhood kids lay on the ground, too injured to move. Three more stood, one holding a baseball bat, another wearing a set of brass knuckles, the third sporting a broken nose. Jake had been walking through his old neighborhood after visiting his foster mother. He'd been heading back for an evening study session at Northwestern University when they'd jumped him.

"What the hell are you doing?" His body was near exhaustion as he struggled to stand up. His long red hair had fallen out of its elastic and hung around his face. "I really don't wanna have to beat the shit out of you guys."

"Dumbass!" shouted the largest of the three punks, kicking him hard in his side before he had a chance to get back on his feet. "Didja really think ya could just come back here without askin' us first?"

"Ya think you're a fuckin' king now that you left, that you're better than us?" added the kid with the brass knuckles, flexing his fists in eager anticipation. "Think again, asshole!"

Jake stepped aside just in time to avoid a brass-knuckled fist to the head, then kicked the boy's legs out from under him. But before Jake could move away, the kid with the broken nose punched him in the kidneys. The hit took his breath away, and he staggered back a few steps.

As he tried to recover, he heard the *whoosh* of a baseball bat slicing through the air, a clumsy attempt that barely missed his head. He dropped and rolled as the kid swung a second time. The bat missed its target once again, but Jake's knee made solid contact with the pavement. Wincing as he got up, he found himself backed up against the grimy brick wall of an alley garage. He was now cornered.

At least I'll be able to see them coming, he thought. *Although if they hit me again, the double whammy of the hit and the wall will hurt a helluva lot more.*

The three boys came at him all at once. He ducked, and one of his attackers' fists hit the wall. He grabbed hold of the bat, but the kid swinging it hung on tightly. The brass-knuckled kid punched him in the hip, and his tenuous grip on the bat lessened. Still, he didn't let go.

The bat kid pulled him off-balance, and the broken-nosed kid shoved him hard against the opposite alley wall. Jake turned as fast as he could, unwilling to leave his back exposed.

That was when he noticed the dark-haired man leaning against the wall a few feet away. Shorter than Jake and slighter, the man had shoulder-length hair and fair skin. His eyes appeared almost black in the fading afternoon light. He wore a wool suit, cut narrow at the torso, obviously expensive. He didn't flinch when Jake hit the wall just a foot away from him.

"Whatcha lookin' at?" Jake demanded, ignoring the other three for a moment.

"You," replied the man, his expression unchanged.

"What are you? Some perv who likes to see guys beat each other up?"

"Hardly." There was a hint of humor in the rich baritone voice. "I came to see you fight, Jacob Anders."

"How d'you know my name?"

"I've been watching you," the man replied as though he were speaking to a child.

"Watching me? You *are* a perv." The thought that the stranger both knew his name and had been watching him left Jake unnerved.

Who is this guy? Drug wholesaler? A pimp? And yet there was an air of sophistication about the man that didn't square with either of those possibilities. For the first time, Jake became aware of how attractive the newcomer was. He pushed the thought out of his mind and focused once more on his opponents.

"You will lose," the man said as if he hadn't even heard Jake's comment.

"I won't lose to these bastards." Jake leaned into the wall, still breathing hard from the exertion. The gangbangers watched the interchange with some amusement, perhaps considering whether they might rob the well-dressed man after they had finished with Jake or wondering whether they should just beat them both senseless.

"I *don't* lose." Jake's face grew hot with anger. He clenched his fists as he pushed himself from the wall.

Who the hell is he, anyway?

"You *will* lose," repeated the newcomer, "because you are angry."

"Nothin' wrong with a little anger to motivate—" Jake's words were cut short by movement from one of the other teens, who ran at him, baseball bat at the ready. Jake snarled and raised his arm to deflect a blow from the bat.

The blow never landed. There was a blur of movement, and the broken bat bounced off the concrete. It was split in two. This was followed by the thud of bodies hitting the pavement. Jake blinked. All three of the boys lay on the ground, unconscious.

Damn, he's fast.

The stranger stood about three feet away from Jake, his suit unruffled. His face was impassive.

"You…?" Jake gasped and looked around in shock. "How the hell did you…?"

"Anger is weakness, Jake," the man replied. "Street smarts, adrenaline, and rage will only get you so far. You must learn to fight with your brain."

Jake looked around once more, and his gaze settled on the broken bat.

I could barely break that thing if I had an hour. He did it in seconds.

"What do you want?" He scowled and tried not to wince as he drew himself up to his full height. Even though he was taller than the newcomer, he was painfully cognizant of the fact that the other man could probably snap his neck in two without breaking a sweat. Still, he was determined not to show his fear.

"I want *you*," the man replied. "Your skills, however undeveloped, are considerable."

"Skills?"

"You are intelligent," explained the man, his eyes fixed on Jake's, "although you choose not to use your intelligence to its fullest potential." Jake scowled again but said nothing. "I can teach you."

"Teach me? Teach me *what*?"

"Teach you to use both your instincts *and* your intelligence."

"I'm doing just fine at the university." Jake dusted off his pants and used his shirt to wipe some of the blood off his face. "They teach me plenty."

"Suit yourself." The man reached into his jacket pocket. "But should you decide that your university studies leave you wanting more, contact me."

Jake took the card from the man's hand.

Trace Michelson, Senior Sales Manager
The Michelson Trust

"Michelson?" mumbled Jake. "Are you…?" But when he looked up, the man had disappeared.

Jake shrugged and pocketed the card.

Three weeks later, unable to contain his curiosity any longer, he contacted Trace.

"THIS seat free?"

The cafeteria was nearly empty. With narrowed eyes, Jake looked up at the tall student carrying the tray full of food. He'd seen the kid around campus, and he was pretty sure they were both in the same Shakespearean Influences in Modern Literature lecture.

"There are plenty of other seats," Jake answered, doing his best to look like he didn't care.

"I want to sit here."

"Yeah. Whatever."

"I'm Greyson Lane," said the young man, who looked to be about Jake's age. "My friends call me Grey."

"Right."

"You're Jake Anders."

"Last time I checked."

"Trace Michelson asked me to introduce myself."

At this, Jake, who'd been working on his statistics assignment and drinking a Coke, looked up. Grey was maybe an inch or two taller than Jake. His broad shoulders, strawberry blond hair, and pale skin called to mind a Nordic god. The kid reeked of middle-class suburbia, and Jake hated him on sight.

"Thought that might get your attention." Grey set his tray down and pulled out a chair, plunking into it and slouching back in the seat.

"What d'you want?"

"I heard you're thinking about interning with the Trust."

Jake did his best not to react.

"I've been working there for a little over a year," Grey continued. "Summers, you know, a few nights a week during the year. You met the old man yet?"

"Old man?"

"Alfred Michelson. Trace's grandfather. Started the company about twenty years ago."

"Nah," replied Jake, trying to keep his expression detached in spite of his growing curiosity.

Jake had only been to the Michelson Trust's offices once, for a company physical and to sign some papers. He hadn't seen Trace since the day Trace had handed him his card. He was beginning to wonder whether he'd be learning "to use both his instincts and his intelligence" as part of Trace's young executive program. Somehow, he had thought Trace had meant something entirely different. After his first visit, Jake had not been back for his "interview," having decided that he didn't care enough about an internship program to waste the little free time he had apart from studying.

"He's a cold one, old man Alfred," Grey said as he stuffed half a hamburger into his mouth and chewed it animatedly. Then, swallowing, he added, "I met him once. Came to watch our first assessments. He took on one of the guys and just about…." Grey trailed off as though he'd said too much.

For a moment, Jake didn't respond. Then, figuring that he didn't really care if Grey thought he was a complete imbecile, he asked, "What does the Michelson Trust *do*?"

Grey blinked, looking slightly hangdog. "They… uh… they're a biotech development company. Implantable computer chips, medical devices, and nanotechnology. That sort of thing."

"Really?" Jake didn't buy a word of it. Nothing about Trace Michelson said "boring scientist."

"Yeah," Grey replied as he made quick work of his french fries. "My girlfriend works there too. She's a biology major. Maybe you've seen her around. Trina Michelson?"

That's *where I've heard the name before*. It had been bothering him since he met Trace nearly two months before. That, and the way Trace seemed to make regular appearances in his dreams.

"Tiny thing? Black hair? Taking statistics?"

His companion nodded.

"Yeah, I've seen her."

"Trace's her brother." Grey took another gulp of his soda and tossed his crumpled napkin on top of his empty plate.

Jake crossed his arms over his chest but said nothing.

"A few of us are working out in the Trust's gym tonight. Why don't you join us?" Grey offered, standing up. "I can use my ID to get you in."

Jake considered the invitation. He didn't much like Grey—too well-behaved for his taste—but he was curious.

What would it hurt? Maybe you can look around while you're there.

"Sure." Jake didn't even glance up from his book.

"I'll meet you in front of the student union around eight," Grey said, waving offhandedly after depositing his tray on the conveyor belt. "I'll drive."

"Yeah," mumbled Jake, watching Grey as he left the room.

THAT evening was full of surprises, not the least of which was the orange Dodge Challenger that Grey drove up in.

"Company car," Grey explained as he gunned the engine with casual aplomb, shifted into gear, and pulled away from the curb. "All the interns get one of their choice. Nice perk."

"Company must be doing well." Jake ran a hand over the leather seats and did his best not to drool.

Grey shrugged. "I guess."

Ten minutes later, they pulled into the empty lot off the main Michelson Trust building. Instead of parking by the front entrance, Grey pulled through the lot and over to a smaller outbuilding. The lights there were dimmer. There were several dumpsters and a stack of rotting wood pallets piled nearby. It reminded Jake of the industrial alleys near his foster home.

What the hell is he playing at?

"Doesn't look much like a gym," he said, thankful he'd strapped one of his favorite knives to his right thigh.

Grey shrugged again. "I guess not." He climbed out of the car, gym bag slung over his shoulder. For a moment, Jake didn't move. "You coming?"

If he tries to rape you, Jake thought, suppressing a snort, *you can always slit his throat.* The thought intrigued him. He found himself half tempted to strangle Grey anyhow. The kid just *oozed* confidence.

"Yeah," he said. He hopped out of the car. He felt the cold edge of the blade pressed against his bare skin through the bottom of the pocket he'd cut out.

Grey pulled a small card from his wallet and swiped it across the electronic sensor near the door handle. There was a mechanical *click* from the lock, and he pushed the door open. Inside was a plainly furnished room with a desk, a chair, and a row of monitors that flickered with pictures of the parking lot and the entryway to the main building. A guard's office, except that there was no guard.

"What are you up to, Lane?" Jake kept his hand on his knife.

"Something bothering you, Anders?" Grey appeared unconcerned. He pushed one of the monitors to the side to reveal a small scanner embedded in the desk. He looked down at the scanner and a beam of red hit his eye.

You've got to be shitting me.

He might be just a street kid, but Jake had watched enough shows on the Science Channel to recognize a retinal scanner when he saw one.

Wonder what other gadgets they have in this place.

The back wall of the guardhouse slid open to reveal a small room beyond. Jake stared openmouthed as Grey replaced the monitor and looked at him impatiently, gesturing to the opening. "Well? You coming?"

Keenly aware that he looked like a complete fool, Jake shut his mouth and, hand still in his pocket, stepped into the room with Grey following at close quarters. The door slid shut soundlessly, and the floor felt as though it were moving downward.

An elevator? Next thing you know, James fucking Bond will turn up.

The room stopped moving and the lights went out. Jake pulled his knife.

"What the hell is going on here?" he demanded, reaching for Grey's neck. There was no one there.

Shit. Shit, shit, shit.

The lights came on, and Jake was nearly blinded by their intensity. He stood on the edge of an enormous room with a high ceiling. In the center of the room was Grey, his back to Jake, talking to someone. Jake walked over and felt his blood begin to boil.

A setup. It was a fucking setup.

And then came the inevitable question: *Why?*

"Thank you, Mr. Lane, for escorting Mr. Anders to his interview," said Trace Michelson, striding over to Jake, who still had his knife pointed in front of him, ready to strike. "I hope he wasn't too much trouble."

"No trouble, sir." Grey smirked, pulled his sweatshirt off, and tossed it onto the floor by the wall.

"Interview? You're joking, right?" Jake lowered his knife a bit and tried not to look into Trace Michelson's piercing eyes.

Shit, he thought. *What are you, some sort of lovesick schoolgirl?* But try as he might, he couldn't help but stare.

"Put the knife away, Jake," said Trace. "You'll fight bare-handed."

"Let him have it if he wants," sniggered Grey. "I can handle it."

"Wait a minute," Jake said with dawning understanding. "I'm fighting *him*?"

Grey laughed outright this time. "You think you can fight Trace Michelson? You've got to be joking."

"I'm not fighting *you*, Lane. I want to fight *him*."

"You're a fucking idiot, Anders. Do you *want* to die?"

"I'll take my chances." Jake narrowed his eyes.

"Enough," said Trace, dismissing them both with obvious irritation. He turned to Jake and appeared to study his face for a moment, then said only, "If you can defeat Lane, I will allow you to fight me."

Jake smirked. "Now you're talkin'."

Trace turned and walked back toward the elevator.

"Hey, wait!" Jake shouted after him. "I thought you were gonna fight me after I finish with him."

"That's exactly what I said," Trace answered as the elevator door closed behind him. "I'll be back then."

It was nearly two years before Jake defeated Grey. During those two years, Grey and Jake sparred almost every night, sometimes bare-fisted, sometimes with knives, sticks, and paint guns. Every night, as Jake headed back to his dorm room, exhausted, his body bruised and bloody, he imagined meeting Trace in the same room and besting him.

And for nearly two years, Jake grew.

chapter three

The Research Project

When the mind comes out of the self, the world appears.

—Ramana Maharshi

JAKE awoke in his hospital bed, the hint of a memory lingering in his foggy brain. He felt the familiar ache in his chest whenever he thought of Trace, as well as a dull ache in his leg. He wasn't sure which was worse.

The painkiller that Dr. Carroll had given him had begun to wear off, but he didn't press the call button to ask for more.

I need to be clearheaded. I need to think. He needed to remember.

"Agent Anders. It's good to see you awake."

Jake struggled to sit up and properly greet the newcomer. "Sir! I apologize that I—"

"There's no need for such formality, Anders," interrupted Charles Haddon. "Please don't sit up. Dr. Carroll tells me that you're still quite weak."

"But, sir—"

"At this moment," said Haddon as he took a seat beside Jake's bed, "consider me simply a concerned colleague, and not the Trust's director." He rubbed his neatly trimmed beard as he spoke these words, and Jake noticed that there were more gray hairs at the man's temples than he remembered. Still, Haddon cut a distinguished figure in his expensive suit and crisply starched shirt. There was no doubt that Charles Haddon had modeled himself on his predecessor, Trace Michelson.

"Of course, sir," Jake replied, his manner stiff. He had spoken to Haddon before, but never like this. Never alone, except for occasional small talk at the company Christmas party or ball game. In spite of his years of service to the agency, Jake still felt uncomfortable around the man.

He wants something.

"Dr. Carroll tells me that you're improving quickly," Haddon said. "I'm pleased to hear it."

"Sir," began Jake, "I still don't understand. Why did Sandoval…?"

"Jason Sandoval was a double agent." Haddon offered this piece of information as if it were almost inconsequential. "The others followed him blindly. Their deaths were… unavoidable."

"Who was the bastard working for?" asked Jake, attempting to school his features into something other than a scowl. He could tolerate a great deal, but having his own colleagues turn on him—*that* was unacceptable.

"We aren't sure. There are rumblings of a new syndicate. A rival, perhaps, to the Trust."

"But—"

"We will discuss this matter more fully when you are feeling better. We're fortunate that we didn't lose you, as well." His matter-of-fact tone foreclosed any further discussion.

"Thank you, sir."

He's hiding something.

"I'm told that you remember nothing of what happened after you stabbed Sandoval," Haddon said after a moment's pause.

"No, sir. I've tried, but I still can't remember."

"I'm also told that you called Trace Michelson's name during the incident."

"Trust no one, Jake," came the Sim's voice in his mind.

"The Sim's program kicked in as I was losing consciousness." He hoped that the explanation would suffice.

"Indeed," Haddon replied. "It appears that the prototype project was a success, then. I'm quite pleased to hear it. There was a great deal of resistance to the idea of the Sims. When you're fully recovered, I'd like you to discuss the experience with Dr. Synchack. Perhaps it will assist him in determining the ongoing viability of the project."

"Of course, sir." Jake shuddered inwardly at the thought of approaching the Trust's head researcher. The idea of patterning the Sims on the thoughts and experiences of former Trust agents had not been Synchack's, and Jake knew that the man would kill to get his hands on his Sim microchip to "study."

Haddon stood up and smiled at him. "I have troubled you too long," he said. "Dr. Carroll will give me no end of grief if I keep you from your rest."

"It's really not a problem, sir," Jake answered. "I feel fine."

"Take some time off, Jake. Finish writing your dissertation. This might be an opportune time to complete it."

"Thank you, sir."

JAKE pulled off his glasses, closed his eyes, and rubbed his hand over his face. He'd been staring at the same page on the computer screen for two hours. Haddon's suggestion of finishing his doctoral dissertation had been followed in short order by the arrival of a large box of documents and a brand-new laptop. It was the last thing that Jake wanted to do, but he needed something to break the monotony. He was sick of being in the clinic, sick of Dr. Carroll's patronizing smiles—sick of being treated as though he were weak, helpless.

Too bad my dissertation isn't on Sim technology, he thought with frustration. He wanted to understand what had happened in Union Station. Frowning, he clicked on the network directory.

```
user id: knifedi
password: !stilettohack4*
```

He scrolled through the directory and clicked on a subdirectory labeled "Research." A long list of research projects popped up on the screen. His gaze was drawn to the one labeled "Resurrection." He was tempted to tap the touchpad.

Synchack will know in a heartbeat that you've accessed the prototype directory.

He'd have to learn more about the Trace Sim another way. He scrolled down and clicked on the project labeled "Light-Emitting Polymers and DNA Detection," his dissertation topic. He then double clicked on a file labeled "Research Results—Analyzed Data."

He thought back to his conversation with the director five days before. It still made no sense. Haddon was hardly stupid. Cold and calculating, but not stupid.

Three agents double-cross him, and he knows nothing? And why aren't his handlers from the CIA knocking at his door for answers?

He remembered his dream—the one in which the Sim had spoken to him. *"Trust no one."*

I'm fucking losing my mind.

Six years before

TRACE had taken over as director of the Michelson Trust after his grandfather's untimely death from a heart attack. Jake remembered Trace's ascendancy in great detail. He knew it had been selfish of him, but he was absolutely livid that, having at last defeated Grey, he wouldn't be entitled to meet Trace in the promised sparring match. Absolutely livid, that was, until Trace showed up in the training gym one night just after Jake and Grey had begun to spar.

"Thank you, Agent Lane," Trace said with his usual cool manner. "You may take the evening off."

Grey, sporting a smirk for Jake's eyes only, nodded and picked up his things. Jake, for his part, just stared at Trace for a moment after Grey had left, not quite comprehending what was happening.

"Well, Agent Anders," Trace said, "you said you wanted to fight me. This is your opportunity."

"I... I...," stammered Jake, keenly aware of the fact that Trace had buried his grandfather only three days before, "I didn't think—"

"No," Trace interrupted, clearly unimpressed, "and that's your problem. You *don't* think. You believed that I wouldn't keep my word to you."

Jake felt surprisingly ill at ease. That was exactly what he *had* thought.

"Don't you want to fight me?" Trace asked when Jake didn't answer.

"Yes... I mean no... I mean, I *want* to fight you," he replied as he struggled to regain his composure.

"Good," Trace said. "Then let's get on with it."

"Just like that?"

Trace frowned. "Come at me, Agent Anders, whenever you're done stalling."

"I'm not—" Jake retorted defensively. Then he ran at Trace, jumped into the air as he spun about, and aimed a heel at his opponent's chest. Trace didn't move away, but grabbed Jake's ankle and flung him backward several feet. Jake lay on the ground watching Trace, panting.

"Is that all you can offer me, Anders?" Trace asked as he raised an eyebrow.

Jake growled and got to his feet, pulled a knife from his pocket, and lunged at Trace. Jake was instantly at Trace's side, his knife just inches from Trace's throat.

Two years ago I would never have been able to get this close to him.

This thought was quickly displaced by a sharp pain as Trace grabbed his wrist and twisted it mercilessly.

Jake's knife clattered to the floor. Spinning about, he kicked Trace in the side. Pleased to have landed a blow, Jake looked up to see Trace studying him intently. Trace still had not moved from his original position.

Jake grabbed Trace's arm and raised a knee to his opponent's abdomen. It felt like steel against his kneecap. Trace moved his left foot a few inches apart from his right to maintain his balance, but appeared entirely unaffected and entirely unimpressed.

Bastard is trying to piss me off, Jake thought with rising anger.

"Show me what you can do, Jake," Trace said, using Jake's given name for the first time that night. "Show me that I wasn't wrong to believe you're better than this."

Jake took a deep breath and closed his eyes for a moment. *Breathe. Remember what you've learned. All that damn meditation stuff must be good for something.... You can't let him rattle you.* He then opened his eyes and lifted his chin as he reassessed his opponent. Two years after their first meeting, he still found it difficult to admit to himself that Trace had been right—that he would never improve if he fought from anger.

For the better part of an hour, Jake attempted every technique he had learned with Grey and his handlers. Every single one failed miserably.

Perhaps hoping to learn more about Jake's abilities, Trace did not strike to incapacitate but only to defend himself from Jake's attacks and to keep Jake moving, forcing him to rethink his strategy again and again.

Throughout it all, Jake couldn't help but marvel at the catlike quality of Trace's movements. Every step the other man made—every flick of his wrist, wave of his arm, turn of his head—every tensing of a muscle appeared to serve a purpose. In spite of himself, Jake was intimidated by the man.

There's no defeating him. He has no weaknesses, and I'm not strong enough to wear him down.

That's when he realized he hadn't been looking at the entire situation from the proper perspective. *He doesn't want me to beat him—he* knows *I can't.* He grinned. He knew exactly what to do. Trace had one flaw: he *believed* that Jake would fail. And Jake would give him just what he expected.

He met Trace's eyes with an expressionless face. Then he spun the knife around in his right hand like a twisted drum major might spin a baton, and grabbed the knife in his left. Narrowing his eyes and frowning in concentration, he ran at Trace with all the speed he could muster. At the last moment, he feinted to the right and aimed for his opponent's left forearm. Out of the corner of his eye, he noted Trace's satisfying look of surprise.

Trace caught hold of and twisted his wrist for a second time, but Jake held tight to Trace's arm as he began to fall. This time, Trace released Jake's wrist and hit him hard across the face with the back of his right hand. Jake winced, almost knocked off his feet by the power of the blow, but he didn't let go of Trace's arm.

"Interesting. Yet you still have learned nothing—" Trace began. Jake ignored him and reached down to his ankle. Trace moved to block what he must have known was a second knife, but with his now freed left hand, Jake turned and punched Trace with all his strength. Trace staggered back several feet. Jake lunged. The blade met its mark, cutting Trace's upper arm and slicing into his bicep. Trace raised an eyebrow, but Jake didn't hesitate: he ran and jumped into the air, hitting Trace in the chest with his elbow.

It's working. I can beat him.

His heart pounded with elation. The feeling was heady. But as he landed back on his feet, Trace grabbed his shoulder. He tried to extricate himself from Trace's grasp, but Trace wrenched his arm behind his back. Something in Jake's forearm snapped.

Shit. Shit, shit, shit.

Trace punched Jake in the temple. Jake fell to the floor and lay there, flat on his back, arm broken, unable to move. The pain in his arm was intense, and he bit his tongue to keep from crying out. He wouldn't show the other man his weakness.

Trace stood over him, studying him with open amusement. A tiny trickle of blood ran down his chin where Jake had punched him and split his lip; his suit was torn where the knife had cut his arm. A dark bloodstain wet the fine wool fabric.

"You chose to sacrifice your strength to win," he said, appearing impressed. "An interesting if dangerous tactic. If I had wanted to, I could have killed you. And yet, in this situation, you knew you had no choice. You did the only thing you could."

"I lost." Jake's voice betrayed his frustration and disappointment. He felt embarrassed to have believed that he could defeat Trace. Childish. Inadequate.

"Yes. You lost. Just as you should. For now, at least." He reached out his right hand to help Jake up.

For a moment, Jake hesitated. The pain in his arm was bad enough to make getting up difficult, but the thought of needing Trace's help to get back on his feet was more painful still.

"Did you truly expect that in two years' time, even with the training we provided, you'd be able to defeat me?" Trace did not withdraw the proffered hand.

The answer, Jake knew, was that he *had* expected just that. But he'd been naïve to hope for victory. Was this yet another lesson that he was supposed to learn?

"No," he said, still breathing hard. "I suppose not." An admission. An acknowledgment of the vast difference between their abilities.

"Good. Apparently you *are* as intelligent as they tell me."

When Jake took Trace's hand, his own felt hot, as if he'd been branded by Trace's singular will. For the second time that night, Jake noticed a flicker of surprise flash through his mentor's eyes, but then it was gone, replaced by the familiar stoic expression. Jake looked away.

The last thing he needs to know about is your teenage crush.

"You will surpass me one day, Jacob Anders," said Trace as Jake got to his feet.

Jake neither got the chance to fight Trace a second time nor to tell Trace the truth of how he felt about him. A little over a year later, Trace was dead, a bullet through his heart.

chapter four

Dead Ends

Man is not born free. He is born to free himself.

—Nanak

"JAKE!" shouted Trina, running over to him as he limped into her office, leaning on a cane. "Dr. Carroll released you from the ward."

Jake winced at her touch and forced a smile. The small office was cluttered with piles of papers. A dozen computers sat on a shelf a few inches above the desk, running simulations. He recognized the project as one they'd worked on together when he was still in graduate school.

"She didn't release you, *did* she?" Trina frowned at him and clicked her tongue against her teeth.

"If I had to stay in that bed one more second…." He leaned against the desk, his jaw tightening as the pain flared once more.

"Sit down," she ordered. She eyed him with concern and cleared a stack of books off one of the chairs.

His leg hurt too much to argue. "Where's Grey?" he asked as he sat. He hadn't seen Greyson since three days before the incident at Union Station.

"On assignment in Europe," she replied with a wistful expression. "Too dangerous for me to tag along, unfortunately. Incommunicado. I haven't heard from him since he left." She laughed, then, in an attempt to hide her worry, added, "Knowing him, he's probably skiing in the Alps."

Jake scowled. He wasn't particularly concerned for his best friend's safety—Grey could more than take care of himself—but Jake had been hoping to learn more about Ares, the only other prototype Sim in use. The Ares Sim hadn't included the memories of a human being as his own Sim had, but Jake knew from his conversations with Trace that the chips shared similar programming.

Patience. You need to keep a low profile.

Trina looked at him. She appeared even more concerned now. "Something's bothering you, I can tell."

"Nah," he lied, then smiled and leaned back in the chair. "Cabin fever. That's all."

"Uh-uh. I don't buy that for an instant, Jacob Anders," she shot back at him.

He said nothing.

She studied him for a moment. Then, pursing her lips, she took a deep breath and said, "I heard that you spoke Trace's name after you were shot."

"Seems like a lot of people heard that."

"Well?"

"It's true," he admitted.

This time, it was she who remained silent.

"Trina," he began, unsure of how to broach the subject, "is it possible…?"

"Possible that he's not dead?" She raised her eyebrows and snorted. "You're joking, right?"

"No."

"Jake," she said, her voice quiet, "he died in my arms. You saw him yourself not long after that."

"But isn't it possible we were wrong? He was the best—"

"He was shot through the heart with an exploding-tip bullet," she said, cutting him off. "My clothes were soaked with his blood. I tried to save him. *You* tried to save him. We couldn't stop the bleeding…." Her voice broke at the memory.

"Maybe he just wanted us to believe he was dead."

Her face reddened and her eyes glittered with anger. "I'm *not* a fool." She faced him down with her hands on her hips. "I know what I saw. I took enough anatomy and physiology classes to know what death looks like. He was dead. He still *is* dead. Dr. Carroll performed the autopsy. The only thing that's left of him is inside of you. That, and an urn full of ashes at the estate."

"I don't think you're a fool. It's just—"

"Do you think he would do something like that to me?" She was fighting for control now, he could tell, but he couldn't let it drop. "Do you think he would put me through that—put *all* of us through that? Even Trace was never *that* cold."

Maybe it was important enough.

Trina sighed, and Jake saw her temper abate. "He was your mentor. You were injured, delirious. You reached out for him. That's nothing to be ashamed of."

He frowned. "I—"

"No, Jake. He cared about both of us too much to make us suffer like that."

"Both?" Jake repeated, surprised by her statement. He'd never thought of Trace as caring for anyone other than his sister. "Maybe you. But me?"

Trina stared at him in surprise. "Of course," she said. "You know, sometimes you really are dense. He cared very much about you."

"He had a funny way of showing it," he answered with a caustic laugh.

"He spoke very highly of you."

"I'm sure he had plenty to say about all of us."

"No." She shook her head. "He hardly ever spoke about any of the other agents. Except maybe Grey. But that wasn't the same."

Jake considered this. The Resurrection project had been Trace's. Was it possible it hadn't been a coincidence that *he* had been the one to receive the prototype Trace Sim chip? For just a moment, he wondered if what he had felt for Trace Michelson hadn't been completely one-sided. Then he laughed inwardly and cast the thought aside.

Let it go. What difference does it make, anyhow, if the man's dead?

There was a knock on the office door, and Ryan Roberts poked his head inside. "Synchack's been looking for you, Anders. Says the director wants you to report to the research lab."

"Yeah, yeah," grumbled Jake as Roberts closed the door.

"Dr. Synchack?" Jake nodded. "What does he want with you?"

"Haddon wants him to study my Sim." He clenched his jaw. It wasn't unexpected, but he'd hoped that Haddon might delay a bit longer.

"Why?" Trina's concern was obvious. Jake knew she didn't trust Synchack either. Nobody at the Trust did, except perhaps Haddon, who had hired the man away from a sister agency under the purview of the CIA.

"Because Haddon, like everyone else, wants to know why the hell I was talking to your dead brother when I passed out," he snapped.

She glared at him.

"Sorry. I didn't mean to jump down your throat like that." He stood up gingerly, biting his tongue at the sharp pain in his leg.

She popped up from her desk and helped steady him. "I'm worried about you, Jake. I've never seen you like this before."

"Like what?"

"I don't know," she said. "Lost, I guess."

"I'm just getting a little cabin fever," he repeated. "Once I get released for an assignment, I'll feel a helluva lot better."

"HOLD still, Agent Anders," Vasalia Synchack instructed him.

Jake tensed, but did his best not to fidget on the examination table.

"I am going to take a reading of your Sim chip."

Synchack approached Jake with a handheld scanner. He paused for a moment about a foot away to press a few buttons on the device, then came closer. The cloying smell of Synchack's cologne made Jake's stomach roil, but before he could complain, a sharp tool cut at his earlobe. Jake pulled his head away.

"What the fuck!" he yelled as he felt the sting and a few drops of blood fell onto his shoulder. "I thought you were taking a reading of it, not digging it out!"

Synchack studied the bloodied chip he held in the forceps. Jake noted the look of unadulterated glee on the researcher's face. Synchack reminded him of a mole—short, balding, and destructive.

Add to that "insane," "untrustworthy," and "creepy as hell."

"I need to test the chip independently of the host."

"How am I gonna train in the simulator without my chip?" Jake demanded.

"You will get this one back after I study it, or I will give you a replacement when you are cleared by Dr. Carroll to begin training again."

For a moment, Jake just sat there, stunned by this pronouncement.

"You may leave, Agent Anders, unless you wish to be my guinea pig...."

Jake got up faster than he thought possible given his injured leg, swearing under his breath as he exited the lab. Once he was far enough down the corridor that he was sure Synchack wouldn't follow, he stopped and leaned against the wall. He absentmindedly rubbed his hand on his shoulder, then, remembering, turned his palm over and frowned at the blood.

You should be fucking happy it's gone.

But he wasn't happy. He had lived with that microchip for the past five years, and he'd come to rely on it, and upon Trace. He knew the chances that Synchack would return it in working order were next to none.

"You will surpass me one day." Trace's words echoed in his mind.

What a joke. Like I ever had a chance, Trace, he thought with bitter resignation. *You didn't stick around long enough for me to try.*

And now, stripped of the last vestiges of the man, he just felt hollow, empty. He took a deep breath, put his weight back on the cane, then hobbled out of the research wing and back to his hospital bed.

"YO."

Greyson Lane stood in the doorway of Jake's apartment, leaning against the doorjamb.

"Grey. I didn't realize you were back in town." He took a pull from the beer in his hand and motioned the other man inside.

"Got in late last night." Grey walked past him and over to the refrigerator, helped himself to a beer, and twisted off the top. "Trina said you wanted to see me."

"Yeah." Jake sat down on the couch across from Grey, who as usual, had taken Jake's favorite chair.

"I heard about your last gig." Grey took a swig of his beer. "Who'd have guessed that asshole Sandoval would try to kill you? Un-fucking-believable. What did the boss man say?"

"Said it might be a rival syndicate," he answered. "A government agency gone rogue, or something like that."

"Interesting." Grey frowned and studied his beer. "As sharp as Haddon is—he wasn't sure?"

"It was bullshit. He knows something he's not tellin'."

"You think he had a hand in it? What happened at Union Station?"

"The guy's as slick as they come. He could be up to his eyebrows in it. Maybe he was lookin' to get rid of Sandoval and Delhomme. You never know."

Grey snorted. "No big loss there. And what's Synchack up to? Trina said the little shit's messing with your Sim. Same deal?"

"I said Trace's name when I blacked out," Jake explained. "I saw him."

"I heard. Trina said you asked her if he might still be alive." He took a sip of his beer, then glared hard at Jake. "What kind of bullshit is that?"

"I was just thinking out loud."

"If you hadn't nearly been killed, I'd probably strangle you myself. What the hell were you thinking, asking her about it? It's taken her years to get over her brother's death."

Jake silently chugged his beer.

He's right, and you damn well know it.

"Where did you get it into your thick head that Trace might not be dead? You saw his body yourself—hell, you were there."

Jake hesitated. "Grey," he asked after a long pause, "do you see the Ares Sim when you sleep?"

Grey, who had gotten up for another beer, replied over his shoulder, "No. Why?"

"It's nothin'."

"Don't give me that shit." Grey grabbed a second beer from the fridge and tossed it to Jake, then set his own bottle on the table and met Jake's eyes. "What's up?"

"Research," Jake answered, looking away so that Grey wouldn't see he was lying. "I was just wondering if the Ares Sim talks to you at all." He had been having regular conversations with Trace even before the incident at Union Station, right up until Synchack had removed the chip. The conversations had started out as dreams, then had progressed to that in-between waking-sleeping time after he had gone to bed.

"Why, do you talk to the Trace Sim?"

"Nah," he lied for a second time. He was pretty sure Grey knew it had been a lie too, from the way the other man frowned at him.

"You dream of Trace?" Grey leaned forward with obvious interest.

"It's *not* what you think," Jake replied, sounding defensive.

"Then tell me what to think."

Jake shifted uncomfortably on the couch. The two men glared at each other.

"Look, Jake," Grey said, his expression now sympathetic, "I know you're into men. I've known it since I first met you. I don't give a shit either."

Jake started in surprise.

Grey laughed. "You can be so dense sometimes. I saw the way you always looked at Trace. I'm not stupid, ya know."

Jake didn't respond. What the hell was he supposed to say to that, anyhow?

"Look," Grey continued, "all I'm saying is that if you and the Trace Sim are… well… you know… it's okay with me."

What the hell. You started this. Now finish it.

"It's not like *that*. We just talk, that's all."

Grey put his feet up on the coffee table and asked, "What do you talk about?"

"Not much, really. We just… *talk*. Sometimes we discuss philosophy, meditation, or politics. We drink tea."

"*Tea?* You're shitting me."

Jake shot Grey a look that was pure bile. "What the hell did you *think* we were doing?"

"I dunno," Grey said. "It's not like I'd have an issue with it if you were… ah… you know…."

"We don't do *that*," Jake retorted.

Grey raised a skeptical eyebrow. Then, probably realizing he'd pushed the issue as far as he could, he said, "I only talk to the Ares Sim in the training simulator and in the field, when I need information. He's like a Google database in my head. No conversation, though. Of course, maybe he does visit me at night, except that I have other things on my mind." He grinned lecherously.

Jake rolled his eyes and shook his head in mock disgust.

Both men drank their beers, and a comfortable silence settled between them. Jake could tell that Grey was waiting to see if he had more to say on the subject of the Trace Sim.

"Since they took the chip out, he's gone." Jake paused as he finished his beer. "I guess I never realized how much I'd gotten used to him being in my head."

I feel empty. Alone.

Jake knew that he must sound as though he were mourning Trace's death all over again. He knew Grey was probably wondering how he would feel if the Ares Sim were removed from his mind, if he'd be just as lost.

Jake got up and pulled another beer from the fridge. His limp was less pronounced now, although his leg still hurt like hell from the physical therapy sessions.

You sound like a sentimental fool.

Grey waved his empty bottle in Jake's direction. "Toss me another," he said.

"If you get shit-faced, Lane, Trina is going to kill ya." Jake snorted as he retrieved a second bottle off the shelf.

"*You're* supplying the alcohol, Anders."

"I'm immune from her wrath, at least for a while."

Grey raised a dubious eyebrow.

Jake pointed to his leg and made a face. "I'm still recuperating. Special dispensation, ya know… I'm all weak and stuff. She feels sorry for me."

Grey tossed his empty bottle at Jake. Jake caught it in one hand without turning around, his reflexes sharp as ever.

"Yeah. Weak like a scorpion, maybe."

"ANDERS, we're releasing you to return to work," the physical therapist told a sweat-soaked Jake a few weeks later. "Get showered and dressed. Dr. Synchack is expecting you in the Sim lab in fifteen minutes."

Jake grunted to acknowledge the therapist, then walked off to the showers, his relief at being released from PT palpable. The torture of the grueling therapy sessions had, however, momentarily taken his mind off his lack of progress at learning anything more substantive about the Resurrection project. Being released from PT meant that he needed to train in the simulator for at least a week before being considered for an assignment. It was better than nothing—he had been off for two weeks, on desk duty for the past four, and he was getting restless. No answers, no missions, no activity other than PT and working on the first draft of his dissertation.

No action makes for a dull Jake. Time to get this show on the road.

The therapist's marching orders and the hot water washed away some of the feeling of helplessness Jake had been experiencing since the incident in Union Station. Despite his newfound strength, he still felt vulnerable, almost weak, without his Sim.

He shut off the water, grabbed the towel, and dried himself off. He was looking forward to the training—to seeing Trace again—in the simulator.

Synchack better not have destroyed that chip... I need it back.

"*Since when do you need a crutch, Anders?*" the Trace Sim asked.

Jake stopped dead as he reached for his boxers.

What the fuck? I shouldn't be able to hear him without the chip....

"*Ever the unbeliever.*"

Jake knew that if he told anyone he was still hearing Trace in his head, he'd be carved up faster than a Thanksgiving turkey at an orphanage.

"*Quite likely.*"

Damn, couldn't you at least have waited until I was in the simulator? Now I'm a fucking lunatic.

"Insanity and brilliance are often partners," answered the Sim.

Determined not to let it rattle him, Jake shook his head clear of these thoughts, finished dressing, and headed for the Sim lab. When he arrived, Synchack was waiting there, head bent over a small stack of paperwork. As he often did, Jake found himself sorely tempted to throttle the researcher.

Little shit.

"Agent Anders, please step into the simulation chamber." Synchack didn't even look up at him but continued to read something on his desk.

"But I have no chip to activate the simulation program," Jake protested.

"Just get inside."

God, I hate that little shit.

Jake stalked into the cavernous chamber, and the door closed with an ominous thud behind him. The red light above the door switched on, indicating that the simulation had loaded. Nothing happened. The room was dark save for the glow of the red light.

Jake waited. Still nothing.

Idiot. Doesn't he remember he fucking dug the chip out of my ear?

Through the window at the front of the observation room, Jake could see that Charles Haddon was now seated next to Synchack. Jake couldn't remember ever having seen the director observe Sim training before.

What the hell is going on?

And then it struck him—both men were waiting to see if the simulation program *would* be activated without Trace's chip. Synchack pressed several buttons and typed information into the computer. Still nothing. Jake continued to stand in the dark, waiting.

They suspect something. But what?

"It appears there is nothing to activate the program, Anders," Synchack said over the speaker.

No shit. I could've told you that, dumbass. No Sim chip, no simulation.

"I've checked all available frequencies," Synchack told Haddon. "No change in brain activity, heart rate, blood pressure, or breathing."

"Anders, please step out of the chamber." Synchack instructed him.

Jake did as he was told. As he exited the chamber, Synchack's daughter and longtime lab assistant motioned him over to the examination table. He hopped up onto it and glanced over to where Synchack and Haddon sat discussing something in low tones. Krista Synchack pulled back his earlobe, reimplanting the chip there so quickly that he only felt the sting when he reentered the simulation chamber a few minutes later.

Damn thing hurts.

The light over the door of the chamber flashed red. This time, he found himself in a holographic town, but there was no Sim to fight.

Bastard damaged the chip.

Through the thick glass, Jake saw Haddon and Synchack speaking animatedly. Jake thought he caught something about a "duplicate chip," and wished his lipreading skills were better— Synchack's thick Romanian accent made him difficult to follow.

Haddon's response, however, was perfectly clear: "Replace the original chip."

It was the first Jake had ever heard about a duplicate Sim chip. He had no doubt now that they were keeping something from him.

Jake was pulled from the chamber once more. Krista ripped the inert chip out of his ear and replaced it with yet another. "Couldn't you test these *before* tearing my earlobe off?" he asked. She said nothing but went about her business as if she hadn't heard him.

This time, when he got up from the table, he felt strangely different, although exactly how, he wasn't sure. It was as if he could *feel* Trace's consciousness, even before he entered the simulation chamber. The door to the chamber closed, and as it did, the red exit light vanished and he was surrounded once more by a holographic town. Trace waited patiently in front of him, just as he had in this universe thousands of times. Jake had no time to think about anything but the exercise.

OUTSIDE the chamber, Charles Haddon was displeased. He wanted desperately to understand how the Sim chip functioned, and he was no closer to that understanding than he had been the day Trace died. Trace's research had been lost—destroyed, most likely. Rebuilding the hard drives of Trace's computers had revealed nothing of interest. Now, nearly six years later, it seemed as if the secrets of Project Resurrection would remain just that: secrets.

He watched the simulation training program as it progressed, and he frowned. The Trust's best and possibly last hope of recreating Trace Michelson's research was at a firm located outside of Raleigh, North Carolina, in a facility in Research Triangle Park, a biotech firm funded by the US government. Who better to send to procure the research than Jake Anders himself? It would be a test of Jake's talent and, most of all, of his loyalty.

JAKE soaked his stiff and aching body in the training facility's hot tub. It never ceased to amaze him that the Sim was just as ruthless and powerful as Trace himself had been. Jake had the cuts and bruises to prove it. Six years after receiving the implant, the holographic simulation had still bested him.

"Your performance was quite adequate," the Sim told him, *"although I sensed that your injury was holding you back. Your hand-to-hand combat sequence, however, was nearly flawless."*

Glad to have you back, Trace, he thought with a sigh.

"I never left you."

At this, Jake just smiled. He was too exhausted to argue semantics with a microchip. Instead, he leaned back against the smooth surface of the Jacuzzi and closed his eyes, letting the heat penetrate his sore muscles.

THAT night, Jake lay in bed, half-asleep. His body was still sore, but it didn't trouble him—he was just happy to be reunited with the Sim and back in training once more.

Trace? he asked, reaching out for the Sim's consciousness.

"Yes?"

Tell me about the Resurrection Project.

"I am not programmed with that information."

Jake sighed.

"Surely you knew that it wouldn't be that simple."

I've tried everything else. It would have been a helluva lot easier if your creator had programmed that information into your database.

"And immeasurably more dangerous for you."

Jake hit his head against the pillow and growled in frustration. *It never ceases to amaze me how irritating you can be.*

At this, the Sim was silent.

Back in the hospital wing, you spoke to me, didn't you?

"Yes," replied the Sim.

You said I should trust no one.

"That would be a wise approach."

Tell me about Charles Haddon.

More silence.

Dammit, Trace! Even if you did die six years ago, you must have had some feeling about him, some reason—

"Even if I did die? And the implication there is—"

Don't dodge the question, Jake shot back angrily.

"I had my concerns."

Jake smiled. Now they were finally getting somewhere. *What kinds of concerns?*

"I am not programmed with that information."

Jake had expected the answer, but he still swore under his breath.

"Your heart rate is increasing. It will accomplish nothing if you remain awake, wasting your energy. You must sleep. The truth will be revealed in time."

Yeah, yeah. Jake knew the Sim was right. He would accomplish little in his current state of mind.

"Breathe, Jake," he heard Trace say, his voice like a caress. *"And grow stronger."*

chapter five

Sniffing Around

To understand the currents of a river, he who wishes to know the truth must enter the water.

—Nisargadatta Maharaj

A WEEK after his last supervised Sim training, Jake was called into the director's office. He had only been in the office a few times since Charles Haddon had taken over as head of the Trust, and he found himself imagining Trace walking into the room and taking a seat behind the sturdy hand-carved cherry desk. But the desk was the only imprint the Trust's former director had left on the room, aside from the image in Jake's mind. He forced the thought away.

"Good morning, Agent Anders," Haddon said. He gestured Jake to the guest chair.

"Good morning, sir." Jake took his seat, willing himself to relax. "You wanted to see me?"

"I have an assignment for you."

Haddon pushed a folder toward him. Jake picked it up and looked over the contents. "When's the briefing?"

"There will be no formal briefing for this assignment."

Although he thought receiving his new orders from Haddon personally was a bit odd, he didn't mention it. He'd expected the usual briefing, after which a mission team consisting of a tech guy, a handler, and an agent would be assembled. The team provided the agent in the field with guidance, ran interference from a distance, and used technology when a lifeline was needed. This was true even of the most top-secret missions. This time, it was apparent that Haddon had something quite different in mind.

"No team?"

"I'm entrusting you alone with this mission, Agent Anders. You are uniquely qualified for this assignment," Haddon replied with a bland smile.

Jake frowned and shuffled through the papers. One word there caught his attention: Resurrection. His expression must have betrayed his surprise. This appeared to please Haddon, who added, "I take it that you're familiar with Project Resurrection?"

"With some aspects, yes."

How could he *not* be familiar with it? Resurrection was the project that Trace Michelson had been working on when he'd been killed—the project that had given birth to the prototype Sims.

"Trust no one, Jake."

"Dr. Synchack believes your Sim may be responsible for your body's extraordinary ability to heal itself. He also believes it's possible that the chip is able to project an image of Trace, which would explain why you might have seen him when you were injured. But the information we have concerning the Resurrection chip is incomplete. We were able to learn little from our examination of the chip."

Jake nodded but said nothing. *He's testing you. He sees you as a potential threat.*

"We have reason to believe that some of the documentation for the Resurrection Project is stored in a government facility," Haddon finished.

"Sir," Jake interjected, "I don't understand why this is a one-man mission. Certainly a team would—"

"If what Synchack suspects about your chip is true, the fewer people who lay eyes on Trace's work, the better. In the wrong hands, this research could endanger the safety of *all* the Trust's agents. We simply can't take that chance."

And there would be fewer people to eliminate if they cause trouble.

"Of course, sir. I understand. What is the mission?"

"Thebes Corporation's Research Triangle Park facility specializes in DNA research and nanotechnology. Your cover will be that you're there to review the facility's DNA research for your dissertation. You'll meet with the facility's senior researcher, Dr. Sarma. Once you have access to their computer network, you will hack into the Project Resurrection files, copy them, and bring them back here."

"And what if the information is the same as we have, Director?"

"Then you, Agent Anders, are the only living link to Trace's work."

There damn well better *be something more to find in Raleigh, or you can bet your ass Synchack's going to use you as his next lab rat, dead or alive.*

THE phantom gray Audi S series roadster hummed along the Kennedy Expressway. The roadway was surprisingly clear. With a rare opportunity to speed, Jake indulged. He knew that with the latest round of budget cuts, the Chicago police were stretched too thin in the neighborhoods to monitor the freeways and that there would be no state police to clock speeders. Golden Earring's "Twilight Zone" blared, and the car shook with the deep bass as Jake approached Cumberland Avenue, the airport extension exit just beyond.

I have no intention of becoming Synchack's lab rat. He bristled, downshifting and feeling the powerful engine race.

"You have good reason to be concerned."

Yeah. Tell me something I don't already know, Trace.

Finding the information about Project Resurrection would not only provide some answers, it would take some of the spotlight off him and focus it on something or someone else.

"If you wanted to be less conspicuous, you could always cut your hair."

What? And look like just another agent? What fun would that be?

HE PULLED into the daily parking garage close to the airport and parked the car. With a click of the key, he activated the high-tech security system he'd personally designed for the vehicle. Then, running his palm gently over the left rear quarter panel to engage the handprint recognition system, he disarmed several of the more dangerous features Synchack had added—standard equipment on all vehicles driven by the Trust's operatives.

He slung his bags over his shoulder and made his way to the terminal, where he waited in a special security line. The ID in his job packet gave him high-security clearance and enabled him to act as a Sky Marshall. With the special clearance, he was permitted to board the plane with the "equipment" he would need for the mission, not the least important of which were the Walther PPK .380 and Colt King Cobra handguns, one of which he carried in his shoulder holster.

He flew first class to Raleigh—the trip was short, just under two hours—but he needed a bit of privacy to review his orders. As the airplane taxied down the runway, Jake opened what appeared to be a small leather-bound notebook: the intel he'd received for the mission. He focused his eyes on the page and engaged a decryption program contained in his Sim to read the information contained within. Anyone else who looked at the paper would see only scribbled calculations, graphs, and text on a plain piece of paper, but Jake saw the layout of the Thebes RTP facility, background and photographs of its staff and director, as well as other information pertinent to his mission. Jake had only thirty minutes to read the information contained on the screen, after which time the data would be wiped clean from the device's memory.

THE plane landed at RDU on time. As Jake headed for the car rental counter, he saw a man with sandy-blond hair and sunglasses holding up a sign that read "Anders."

My Spidey-senses aren't tingling. What d'you think, Trace?

"The man is from the facility you are here to visit. Jonas Foster."

So it's safe?

"Yes, but he's no limousine driver."

Hardly a surprise. No doubt Foster also knew that Jake wasn't just the average doctoral student.

Jake approached Foster, who flashed him a broad smile. "Jacob Anders," Foster said, peering at him through a pair of green sunglasses. "For a moment there, I thought you were going to walk right by me. I'm Jonas Foster."

"I'm sorry. I didn't realize I'd be getting a ride to the facility. I'd reserved a rental." Jake grasped the man's extended hand and shook it.

"Of course," Foster replied, unfazed. "However, Dr. Sarma is quite particular about how she treats her visitors. You'll be staying at the facility in the guest quarters. She didn't want you wasting time going back and forth to a hotel, given how short your stay is."

"I wouldn't want to impose," Jake answered.

"You needn't be concerned, Mr. Anders. Tanvi—Dr. Sarma— wouldn't have it any other way." He gestured to the curb where a black Mercedes limo waited, idling. "This way, please."

"MR. ANDERS, please wait here for Dr. Sarma." The lobby receptionist ushered Jake into a nicely appointed room lit with natural light. Jake sat in a comfortable leather chair. He had to wait only a minute or two before a woman walked into the office from another door. She wore a lab coat and hangtag, her dark burgundy hair pulled into a high ponytail.

"Ah, Mr. Anders, I see that you've been issued your photo ID," she said. "I'm Tanvi Sarma. Good to meet you."

Jake stood and shook the researcher's hand—for such a petite woman, she had a surprisingly strong grip. "Thank you for taking the time to meet with me. I realize you must be quite busy."

She smiled, taking the measure of him and raising a perfectly sculpted eyebrow in tacit approval. "Your reputation precedes you, Mr. Anders. I've heard about your work with DNA engineering. It could open the door to some new technologies in identity protection. I've also heard that you've developed a mean car security system."

"Thank you," he replied, masking his surprise with a smile.

"Nor is Tanvi Sarma just a researcher," the Sim noted with obvious pleasure. Jake had to suppress a chuckle—sometimes the chip's programming was just a little too realistic for comfort.

"I trust you found your accommodations satisfactory."

"Very much so. Thanks again for your hospitality."

"Good. Then let's begin with a tour of the Thebes RTP facility. You'll be here for a few days, and I want you to feel at home. Follow me, please." She pointed him toward an elevator outside a set of glass doors, and they descended several levels underground. Jake's room was located on the same level, although without a hangtag ID, he'd been unable to explore the research area when he'd arrived.

After exiting the elevator, they walked down a long corridor and stopped in front of another set of glass doors. Tanvi pressed her key card to the scanner by the door and led him through a maze of winding passageways to the main research facility, where she pointed out several labs and described some of the projects they were working on.

"This facility is dedicated exclusively to DNA research and nanotechnology—different applications and uses for both," she explained as Jake glanced with interest into the labs.

"As I mentioned earlier, Mr. Anders, your reputation precedes you. If you're ever interested, I'd be more than happy to have you join my research staff."

"Are you trying to recruit me, doctor?"

"Of course." She grinned at him, her amber eyes twinkling. "Are you happy with your career, Mr. Anders?"

"Please call me Jake, Dr. Sarma," he replied with his usual affable grin. "And yes, I *am* happy with my job."

"Call me Tanvi."

"Of course, Tanvi."

They continued around the maze of labs.

No wonder they were so willing to share their research. Red rover, red rover, let Jake come over....

"Indeed," noted the Sim.

"And this," she said as they turned a corner, "is the nanotech lab." She opened a heavy steel door and motioned him inside. "My pride and joy. I hear you dabble a bit in the field, as well."

"I worked with the Trust's former director on some nanotech projects," he replied, looking for her reaction. "I also did some research with a colleague of mine, Dr. Greyson Lane, several years ago. I'm hardly an expert, though."

"You're too humble. From what Trace told me, you're more than just proficient in the field."

"You knew Trace?" Jake was starting to wonder with whom he should be more irritated—Charles Haddon or the Trace Sim.

Why the hell did you keep that one from me?

"You never asked, Jake," the Sim replied in a dismissive tone.

"Of course I knew Trace," laughed Tanvi, closing the door behind them. "He was, after all, my first cousin."

"I had no idea," Jake replied.

You are so dead, Trace!

The Sim did not answer.

Tanvi introduced Jake to some of the scientists at work outside a sterile enclosure that took up more than half of the room. He smiled at each of them, shaking their hands and thanking them for allowing him to review their work. He committed the layout of the lab to memory, including the locations of all points of access. The computer system, he noted, appeared to be stand-alone, making it more of a challenge to hack. The sterile room was another thing entirely—behind the polarized glass, it was difficult to make out anything beyond the vague outlines of people moving about inside.

I guess I shouldn't be surprised she didn't offer to take me in. They're probably worried I might make off with proprietary information about the production process.

"With your badge, you now have access to everything in this facility with the exception of the classified archives," Tanvi explained. "Those are Level Three, top-secret clearance accessible only."

After leaving the nanotech lab, they passed by a windowless room marked "Authorized Personnel Only." Jake guessed it housed the classified computer archives Tanvi had alluded to. He made a quick assessment of the security system as she showed him the research archive room across the hall, and noted the types and locations of the computerized locks. These included retinal and voice-pattern recognition, full handprint verification scan, and badge swipe.

"Difficult, but not impossible to defeat," the Sim said.

I doubt that it can be accessed from an external server, Jake replied, *but I can try.*

After they finished their tour of the research labs, Tanvi escorted Jake back to the guest quarters. "I'm told that you appreciate a good workout facility." The edges of her mouth quirked upward in silent challenge. "I think you'll find that ours is more than up to your high standards."

Jake didn't miss a beat. "I plan to visit it soon."

"Perhaps we could work out together, then. I'm always on the lookout for sparring partners who can keep me on my toes."

"I have to warn you, I fight no-holds-barred," he quipped with a sly wink.

"Just how I like it! Tomorrow afternoon, then? Around four o'clock?"

Jake nodded, intrigued by her offer. He'd been joking, of course, but he relished the idea that he might find an equal in her.

"She is not an opponent to be taken lightly," Jake heard the Sim say.

You'd probably like to see her beat the shit out of me, wouldn't you?

Again, the Sim did not answer.

"Perfect," Tanvi replied with a bright expression. "But for now, why don't you let me take you to dinner with a few of the scientists you'll be working with."

DINNER was a pleasant affair. Jake was able to glean a few helpful bits of information from his companions without being too obvious. That the researchers had heard of him and knew of his work made them a bit more forthcoming with information. Afterward, Jake returned to the facility to do some nighttime recon, stopping first at his room and changing into his sweats under the pretext of wanting to work out. As he made his way to the gym, he passed by the archives. He needed to plant a few devices—devices that could provide him information without risk of detection.

As he walked by the archive door, he coughed and grabbed the small towel he'd tossed over his shoulder to cover his mouth. With a flick of his wrist, he threw the towel back over his shoulder, launching the first of three tiny devices into position above the archive door. Half as big as the nail on his little finger and wafer thin, it blended in with the grain of the wood and was nearly invisible. He cleared his throat, planting a second device with a view of the door from across the hall. It too found its mark. He placed the last device on the ceiling, covering this time with a noisy flick of the towel back over his shoulder. Assured that the devices were securely set, he headed toward the gym. As he walked, his phone vibrated to confirm that the bugs were all up and running. He would go work out while he waited for the information he needed.

chapter six

Eyes Wide Shut

Tomorrow's wind blows tomorrow.

—Koji

Eight years before

"NICE place." Greyson Lane carried a large box in his arms as Jake held the door to the apartment open. More boxes were stacked in the living room, which was devoid of furniture but for a comfortable recliner and a bookshelf. "You might want to get a couch, though."

"Shut up," Jake shot back. "I've ordered a couch. It'll be here tomorrow. Figured with the extra money I'm making at the Trust now that I'm outta school, I'd buy a nicer one. Besides, I've seen your place, remember? Anyone who calls a futon a couch shouldn't be giving decorating advice."

Grey snorted. "It's not like I spend a lot of time at my place."

"Thank God for Trina. At least *she* has taste." Jake pulled the receiver from his stereo system out of a box and set it on the bookshelf.

"Have you seen her brother's penthouse on the lake?" Grey put the box down and kicked the door shut behind him.

"No." Jake cut the top off another box and began to unpack the CD player. Grey brought one of the large speakers over. He looked surprised.

"Really? I thought you'd've been over there a bunch."

"Why would you think that? It's not like Trace and I are friends." Jake avoided his friend's gaze and started to plug the speaker wires into the back of the receiver. Truth was, he was pretty much convinced that Trace Michelson didn't like him. He'd heard some of the more experienced older Trust "executives" talk about dinner parties Trace hosted at his lakefront apartment, but he'd never been invited.

"I'm not his friend either," Grey countered, "but I've been there."

Great, Jake thought with a scowl.

"That bothers you, doesn't it?" Grey asked as he retrieved the other speaker from the hallway.

"No," lied Jake. "Why should it?"

Grey laughed. "I see how you look at him. Like the guy walks on water or something."

"Fuck off."

"Seriously. You got some real hero worship going on, ya know?"

Jake shifted his position and avoided Grey's gaze. "That's bullshit. Besides, everyone admires the guy."

"Yeah, but it's different with you," Grey replied, goading Jake. "You like geeks?"

"He's not a geek," Jake protested a bit too defensively. "No geek is that smooth."

"The guy graduated from UNC Chapel Hill at nineteen."

"Carolina?" This surprised Jake, who'd figured Trace had gone to some snooty eastern school like Harvard or Yale.

"Yeah. Got his MD/PhD at Duke in biotechnology."

"All right. So he's a sophisticated geek." Jake laughed and walked over to the fridge, pulled out two beers, and tossed one to Grey, who was still sitting on the floor.

"Heard you got assigned to special ops."

"Team Three." Jake breathed an inward sigh of relief that Grey had moved on to another topic. "With that asshole Pilkington and his buddy, what's his name…?"

"Grant Schaeffer," Grey supplied.

"Yeah, that's the other asshole."

"At least he can shoot." Grey took a pull on his beer. "Pilkington'd have a hard time hitting an elephant if it was three feet away from him."

"So I heard." Jake shook his head. "What's it like?"

"Going on a mission?"

Jake nodded.

"It's okay." Jake could tell that Grey was holding back.

"You ever killed someone?"

"Yeah, sure." Grey shrugged. "No big deal." He took a big swig of his beer, then walked to the fridge for another.

"Oh." Jake tried not to react. He knew, of course, that it was part of their job. He'd heard the spiel a hundred times; it was part of why he'd signed up for the work. The special ops unit was responsible for identifying and eliminating rogue biotechnology operations worldwide. "What's it like?" he added after a pause.

"You really wanna know?"

"I guess," Jake admitted. Even though they had spent almost every night together sparring in the Trust's gym, they had never talked about Grey's missions. "I mean, I know what we're supposed to do…."

"I don't mind when it's the sickos who do the experiments on people, you know," Grey tossed off with a casual wave of his hand. "Fuckers deserve it." He laughed, but this time there was a hard edge to the sound. He twisted the cap off a bottle and took a few swigs. "It's the others… you know… the victims. They're the ones who get to you."

Jake's trainers had never tried to hide that part of the job. He understood that sometimes, if a victim of an experiment couldn't be treated, euthanasia was the only humane option.

"It gets easier," Grey offered. He walked over to the balcony and stepped out into the warm spring sunshine. "At least, the doing part does." He took a deep breath and leaned on the railing, his eyes focused off in the distance.

Jake followed, unsure of how to react. "You ever think about doing research instead?"

"You're shitting me." Grey turned and stared at Jake, wide-eyed. "I'd shoot myself if I had to spend all day in the lab like Trina. The old man wants me to finish my PhD by the end of the year. I figure I'll do it, since he's paying for it. But after that, I'm going full-time in ops. I'll still get plenty of lab time, anyhow, between gigs."

IT WAS only a few months later that Jake was called into Trace Michelson's research lab. He received word that he was to meet Trace in an outbuilding on the Trust campus. Until that meeting, Jake had never been inside the small building, and he needed to ask directions from one of the administrative staff to even find it.

Still relatively new to the Trust and having just begun his graduate work in biomedical engineering at the Illinois Institute of Technology, Jake was only now being sent on high-level missions. This was less a reflection of Jake's abilities in the field than of his need to complete his undergraduate classwork.

Jake saw Trace nearly every day, but he still felt ill at ease around him. Since his "interview," and with the exception of their sparring match, Jake had rarely been alone with his mentor.

"You lookin' for me?" Jake asked, leaning against the doorway to the lab and peering inside at Trace who sat, head bent over a large microscope, jotting down notes.

Trace looked up and frowned, his piercing blue eyes meeting Jake's own with obvious impatience for Jake's lack of deference. Of course, it was for this reason alone that Jake refused to address the man by his formal title, as was expected of him. He might have been intimidated by Michelson, but he would damn well *not* show it. He had purposely changed out of his suit and into a pair of faded jeans and a T-shirt for the meeting.

As always when he saw Trace, he felt the distant thrum of desire course through his body. From where he stood, he could see the outline of Trace's muscles through the soft fabric of his shirt. He found himself imagining what it might be like to touch Trace's soft skin beneath the silk or to glide his tongue over the slight indentation at the base of his neck. The faint scent of Trace's cologne hung in the air, and he swallowed hard as he fought his body's physical response.

"Yes." Trace put down his fountain pen and capped it, studying it with a thoughtful expression. "There's something I wish to discuss with you, Agent Anders. Please have a seat." He gestured to a steel stool across the table.

Jake obliged and eyed Trace warily. "Look," Jake began, "if this is about the little *disagreement* I had with that bastard Pilkington the other day, it's really—"

"I have not called you here to discuss your—" Trace paused for a moment and sighed. "—*differences* with the other executives."

Jake wondered what other faux pas he might have committed to deserve an audience with the high and mighty Trace Michelson. "Yeah, well, he deserved the broken arm, anyhow."

"I don't doubt that," Trace answered, much to Jake's surprise. He nodded to Jake's arm, which was still in a sling from their sparring match, and added, "Misery loves company, it appears."

For a moment, Jake was speechless. Had the other man been attempting *humor*? But when he searched Trace's face, his expression was unreadable.

"I brought you here," Trace continued, "to determine your interest in participating in a new project of mine."

"Project?" Jake took in their surroundings at last. Until then he'd been too busy studying Trace Michelson to pay attention to much else. He found it difficult not to stare at the man, and he hoped he wasn't being too obvious. Sexual orientation wasn't exactly a topic for casual banter at the Trust. Not that he cared what anyone thought of his attraction to men, but still....

"Wow," Jake marveled, nearly drooling. "What're you doin' in here? Creating your own Frankenstein monster?"

In one corner of the room was digital X-ray equipment, in another, several large glass cabinets fully stocked with chemicals, growing media for biological samples, a large centrifuge, and an examination table. Nearly half of the room was walled off to create a sterile environment, and it too was fully stocked with equipment. Just behind a glass wall at the back of the large room was an outrageously expensive electron microscope, as well as sterile isolator equipment for sample preparation.

As he watched Jake take in the room, the corners of Trace's mouth edged upward, the closest thing to a smile Jake had ever seen on that handsome, brooding face. "Perhaps."

"I'm in," Jake responded without hesitation. He had no idea what he'd just signed up for, but he didn't care. He trusted Trace and admired the man on a level that bordered on hero worship, even if he'd never admit that to anyone, let alone Trace Michelson himself.

"Don't you want to hear what you've just signed up for?"

"Yeah, sure." Jake stood up and walked over to one of the tables covered with scribbled notes and equipment, doing his best to look nonchalant. "I'm guessin' this has somethin' to do with the current Sim chip program."

"And how did you arrive at that particular conclusion?"

At this, Jake picked up a scrap of paper and turned back to Trace. The intelligence he usually hid from the outside world now shone brightly in his eyes and on his face. "You've found a way to create true AI—artificial intelligence—a sentient chip."

"I'm impressed." Trace's eyes sparkled with amusement.

"It's nothin'," Jake drawled, slipping back into his street personality. "So when do we get started?"

"Soon. Dr. Carroll is running the final tests on the prototypes."

"Prototypes?" Jake asked with surprise. "There's more than one?"

"Yes. You will receive the second."

At this, Jake frowned. He was pretty sure just who the first to receive the implant would be, and he felt as though he'd come up second best yet again.

"The pecking order of recipients has nothing to do with your importance to this project," Trace said, clearly picking up on Jake's disappointment. "Greyson Lane's chip will be… different."

Jake laced his fingers behind his neck and leaned back on the stool, trying to appear unconcerned. Inwardly, he felt like a jealous child vying for the attention of a favorite teacher.

"We'll begin work in a few weeks," Trace continued. "You'll receive a series of Sim chips and inoculations and report for regular testing in the lab with Dr. Carroll. I anticipate that the final prototype will be ready in about a year."

"*A year?*"

"Patience, Jake, is truly a virtue." Trace ran long fingers through his hair and sighed. "I promise you won't be disappointed with the final product."

But one year later, Trace was dead, and it was Dr. Carroll who implanted the chip into Jake's ear and gave him a battery of inoculations she claimed Trace insisted were necessary "to counteract any immunosuppressive response" to the implant. What Jake didn't realize until the moment the chip became live was that "Project Resurrection" was the essence of Trace Michelson himself, imprinted upon the prototype.

Dr. Carroll smiled when she gave him the Trace Sim. "I only wish that he could have lived to see this day, Jake," she said in a moment of surprising emotion. "He would have been so pleased."

In the end, of the three dozen executives who led dual lives as high-risk operatives, only a dozen received the sophisticated microchip technology that permitted them to train in the simulator. And with the possible exception of Greyson Lane's Ares chip, none of them even approached the sophistication of Jake's Sim. It was Trace Michelson's masterpiece.

chapter seven

Information, Please!

Truth has no path, and that is the beauty of truth; it is living.

—Krishnamurti

"DAYDREAMING?" came a woman's voice from over Jake's shoulder.

"Hmm?" Jake started and looked up to see Tanvi Sarma standing over him. "Yeah, I guess I was."

"It's four o'clock," she announced. "I'll be waiting for you in the gym. I'll bring my first aid kit in case you should sustain any serious injuries."

"Not on your life." Jake stood up and stretched.

Ten minutes later, Jake walked into the gym wearing a pair of baggy sweats and a fitted T-shirt, his hair tied in a ponytail. With the exception of Tanvi and a lone figure who sat at the top of the row of bleachers at the far end, the huge gym was empty.

"Spectators?" laughed Jake. "You *do* take this seriously!"

"Jonas likes to watch." She winked at him.

"Really?" Jake pulled off his sweatshirt and considered the double-entendre.

"Frankly, I like the show already," she purred. Her gaze lingered on his torso, then followed the reddish hair on his abdomen to where it disappeared beneath his sweatpants.

"She hasn't changed," murmured the Sim, much to Jake's surprise.

It's reassuring to know your programming isn't completely worthless.

"Weapons?" Tanvi asked.

"Your choice," he replied.

"Swords, then."

"Swords?" Jake knew next to nothing about swords.

"You said it was my choice," Tanvi countered with a healthy grin.

"All right."

What do you know about swordplay, Trace? he asked the Sim hopefully.

"I am schooled in both European and Asian weapons and techniques" was the Sim's confident response.

She led Jake to a small room filled with weapons of varying shapes and sizes—all of them lethal in their own right. "I'm impressed," he said, perusing a rack of swords near the far wall.

"Thanks. I'm a collector. I store all my weapons here—it's much easier than dealing with permits and nonsense, you know."

He chuckled, then turned back to the rack. There were at least thirty swords from which to choose, including several that looked like modern takes on an old theme, fashioned using the latest in metal alloys. Jake ran his fingers across several, considering them. He picked a few up, felt them in his hands, and replaced them on the rack. When he walked around the back of the rack, he was immediately taken by an unusual weapon near the bottom. The sword had a red handle and sheath with a rectangular bronze hilt. He picked it up and eased his fingers around the grip.

"I'll use this one," he said.

"You have no idea what to do with it," he heard Trace say.

That's why I have you to help me, O Wise One.

"Hmm."

"Interesting choice." Tanvi pursed her lips in eager anticipation. She, in turn, picked up a shorter sword: simple, Asian in design, and well tailored to her small body.

"That is a wakizashi," Trace explained. *"Often used to accompany a larger katana in feudal Japan."*

And my blade?

"I'm not sure. Probably also Japanese, although I do not recognize it. Similar to a traditional katana, with the exception of the jagged protrusions."

Great. This should be entertaining.

"I have little doubt," Trace responded.

They walked back to the large room in silence, Jake moving his weapon about to get the feel of it.

"Swordplay is no different from what you have already learned," Trace explained. *"You must analyze your opponent's capabilities and exploit her weaknesses."*

Simple enough.

"But of course, she has very few weaknesses to exploit," the Sim added sardonically.

Great.

"Ready?" she asked him.

"No protective gear?"

"More fun this way. Unless, of course, you're worried I might hurt you?" He could see the challenge in her eyes.

He shrugged. "I trust you not to kill or maim me." He hoped his trust wasn't misplaced.

"Ready?" she called again, this time from the other side of the gym.

"Ready," he replied, doing his best to focus on the task at hand.

They ran toward each other, meeting in the center of the room as their blades rang with a resounding *clank*. She pivoted gracefully on one foot, as did Jake. Again their swords met, the metal singing throughout the room.

"Not bad, Jakey," she laughed as she pushed away from him and slid back several feet.

This time it was Jake on the offensive, taking several steps forward and swinging his blade parallel to the floor. She jumped backward, easily avoiding the razor-sharp tip. But before he could reset for his next attack, she had moved like lightning to his side, striking him in the arm and pulling back her weapon. Tiny beads of blood formed a line across his bicep.

"You're going easy on me," he said with a smirk. "You could easily have cut my muscle."

"I could have. But I'm having fun. I didn't want to make you look bad for trusting me. Besides, you need a few minutes to figure out what to do with your weapon."

It was Jake who laughed this time. "Is it that obvious?"

"That you have no clue how to fight with swords? Of course. But that's exactly why I chose to fight with them. I wanted to see how good you are at improvisation."

This revelation drew another attack from Jake, who crouched low and swept across the floor with his blade. She jumped over it as if she were playing a child's game of hopscotch.

"You won't touch me like that, Jake," she taunted. With a sharp cry, she jumped and kicked him in the chest. The blow did not set him off-balance, but it did force him to release one hand from the heavy sword. Seizing the opportunity, she kicked him once more, and his katana fell to the ground. She raised her weapon to his face. With his bare hand, he grabbed it and pushed it away.

"Unfortunate," he heard the Sim say.

Better my hand than my face. What the hell was I supposed to do, let her cut me?

"Hardly," Trace replied. *"You should never have let her get close."*

The Sim was right and he knew it. He was fighting like an amateur, not the professional that he was. Regaining his focus once more, he looked over to where the sword had fallen, then dove to pick it up again, dodging her blade as it whizzed by his ear so fast that it hummed.

"Use the weapon, Jake."

I'm trying!

He gritted his teeth and wiped his bloody hand on his pants, then grabbed the handle of the katana as hard as he could, placing his left hand on top and pressing hard to stem the bleeding in his palm. That was when he noticed the tiny indentation on the top of his weapon's grip.

"Curious," the Sim said.

What does it do?

"I believe it releases the joints that compress the blade."

Releases? You mean this thing extends?

"Precisely."

Did you know this before?

"I suspected it."

You might have told me. That's your job, isn't it?

"My job is to assist you with your work. This is pleasure."

Is that what you call it? Jake shook his head.

"What's so funny, Jakey?" Tanvi taunted. "You're not looking so great to me. I'd hate to carve up that pretty face of yours."

"It's nothing. I always get beat up before I figure out what the hell I'm doing," he answered with a smirk. "That's how your cousin taught me, anyhow."

"How sweet." She swung her blade within inches of his chin.

He was ready this time. He grabbed her left wrist and twisted it hard. She pulled away from him after a moment, but the damage was done—the injury would slow her down.

"Nicely done," Trace commented.

Jake ignored the Sim, instead kicking Tanvi in the side. She sprang away with little effort, then reset herself for another attack with her weapon.

Using martial arts maneuvers and his sword, Jake engaged her for several minutes more. He could see the sweat bead on her brow, and he knew that he was making progress. After a fourth pass at her with his weapon, she withdrew to reset for another attack.

Perfect.

Jake didn't hesitate; he met her sword, their wrists making brief contact. She was strong, but not strong enough to keep him in place. Instead, she ducked underneath the weapons and aimed for his side. He winced as the blade cut his waist, but he did not cede his position. This was exactly what he'd planned to do—make her believe that he was becoming tired, vulnerable.

"You do seem to enjoy that tactic," Trace commented dryly. *"You've gotten better at it since we fought years ago. A consummate actor."*

Again their blades scraped against each other, and again their bodies twisted about in a dangerous dance. Each time she successfully defended the attack, and each time they came back face to face, their eyes locked, faces set in a grim war of wills.

"Now, Jake!" Trace prompted.

Instead of meeting her blade, Jake backed off and pressed hard on the indentation in the grip. He swung his sword downward. Tanvi dropped to the ground and rolled to the side. Jake pulled back on the blade at the last second to avoid hitting her. It missed her by an inch, striking the floor and creating a foot-long rut in the concrete a half an inch deep. He had won.

"Nice," she said as he put his hand out to her to pull her up off the floor. "But I thought you fought no-holds-barred."

"I didn't want to kill my host," he quipped, examining his cut palm with interest. "That'd be inexcusably rude."

That wasn't so bad, he thought, quite pleased with himself.

"She wasn't fighting at her full strength," the Sim said.

Really? Could've fooled me.

"Apparently she did *fool you. I, on the other hand, know of what she is capable."*

Why would she have held back?

"I don't know, although I can speculate."

Please do.

"She wants something from you."

Other than recruiting me?

"Yes."

"Trace wasn't joking about you." Tanvi chuckled as she dusted herself off. She pulled a first aid kit from the wall, took his injured hand, and wiped the gash there with disinfectant.

"He spoke about me?"

"Yes," she replied. "Several times. Told me he'd recruited you. Said you were 'promising', I believe."

"Seriously, Tanvi, I really *am* happy where I am."

She just raised an eyebrow and grinned. "I wasn't talking about him recruiting you into the Trust. I meant that he recruited you for Project Resurrection."

Jake tried not to show his surprise. The last thing he'd expected was for her to raise the topic of Trace's research. And that was when he understood why she hadn't fought him full out—why she had even asked him to fight at all.

She needed a place away from prying eyes where she could let me know.

She looked up at him. "Gotcha, didn't I?" She laughed and strode over to the stands where Foster still sat, perfectly still. "Oy! Jonas! Can you toss me that thing?"

Jonas Foster stood up and reached into his pocket, then threw something down to her so fast that Jake could barely follow it. She caught it with one hand behind her back without even looking.

Nice.

"I have something for you," she said. "Something I believe you came to North Carolina to retrieve."

"I don't know what you're talking about," Jake said, refusing to take the bait.

"Of course you do, Jakey." She opened her right hand to him. In it lay a silver jump drive. "These are the classified files on Project Resurrection for you to take back to your boss."

LESS than twenty-four hours after Tanvi had handed him the jump drive, Jake sat in Director Haddon's office waiting to be debriefed. As always, the office was immaculate, almost antiseptic. It reminded Jake much of Charles Haddon himself—hard to read and distant. Jake looked over at the windowsill, remembering the tiny bonsai cherry tree that used to sit there years ago, when the office bore the distinctive stamp of its previous owner.

Those were different times.

Jake had turned the computer files over to the Trust, as Tanvi Sarma had clearly expected him to. Despite his reservations about Haddon, Jake's allegiance was still firmly with the organization into which Trace had recruited him. That allegiance was hard-won, but once he'd made a commitment, he was loyal to a fault.

"Jake," said Haddon, striding into the room holding a stack of paperwork. Jake stood. "Please, have a seat. We needn't stand on formality."

"Thank you, sir."

A small dark-haired woman entered the room bearing a tray with a simple pottery tea set on it. "Your tea, Director Haddon," said Cathy Smyth, Haddon's assistant.

"Thank you, Cathy," Haddon replied with a pleasant smile. "Tea, Jake?"

This is a first, thought Jake.

"Indeed," the Trace Sim added.

"Yes, thanks." Jake wondered what approach the director would take after having read the report about his trip to Raleigh.

Haddon poured two cups of steaming tea and handed one to Jake.

"Thank you," Jake said as he took the cup and began to sip the hot liquid. He rolled the tea around on his tongue as he'd seen Trace do years before. It was exquisite.

Can't fault him for his taste.

"Really? The man never drank tea until after my death."

"I saw your report," Haddon said. "Sounds like it was relatively easy to obtain the files."

"I ran into a few snags." Not quite a lie, but not the complete truth either. For now, at least, he would keep the specific details of what had happened with Tanvi to himself. "Nothin' I couldn't handle."

"Good, good," said Haddon. "Dr. Synchack is analyzing the data now. It appears there are three encrypted files on the drive. Perhaps with the Trust's mainframe decryption programs, he'll have more luck than you did reading their contents."

"From my brief review of the files," Jake replied, "I wasn't able to identify the type of encryption used. I didn't find any decryption programs in the Thebes computer databases, either." This was completely true. He'd spent hours reviewing the documents on the thumb drive before his plane had left Raleigh, but to no avail.

"Quite unfortunate," Haddon replied. "I'd like you to check in with Vasalia when you have an opportunity. Perhaps the information needed to unlock the files is stored in your Sim's database."

"I'm happy to assist Dr. Synchack if it will help." Jake was just thankful that Haddon hadn't suggested they remove the Trace Sim for a second time.

"Good, good." Haddon put his cup down on the table and stood up. "Then I look forward to hearing the results of your work soon."

Sensing that he'd been dismissed, Jake stood as well and said, "Thank you for your time, sir. I'll keep you up to speed on our progress."

Progress, however, proved elusive. Try as he might, Jake was unable to locate any information in the Sim's database to unlock the encrypted files. The Trace Sim insisted that he wasn't programmed with information relating to decryption of any sort, with the exception of the files loaded from the Trust's own computers.

Leaving the office at midnight after Synchack summarily dismissed him for being "a pest," Jake worked out for a little over an hour in the Trust's gym, then headed back to his apartment. He was thoroughly exhausted and thoroughly frustrated by their lack of progress at reading the files. He downed a beer for good measure and lay down in his bed. Sleep was nearly as elusive.

At this rate, that bastard Synchack'll pull the chip out of my ear again.

"You're tired, Jake."

And you're stating the obvious, Jake retorted, irritated with the Sim's seeming lack of concern regarding the potential risks involved in Synchack's lack of progress. *You, of all people, must have anticipated this. And yet....* He rubbed his forehead and frowned. *Trace?* he said after a moment.

"Yes?"

You—Trace, I mean—did expect me to get my hands on the computer files, didn't he?

"Yes."

Now we're getting somewhere.

"In what way?" the Sim asked.

Jake shook his head. *You know damn well what I'm getting at.*

"Feel free to educate me."

You must have planned for this, if you died.

"It seems likely."

And in spite of that, you found no decryption keys in your database.

"That's true. I found no decryption key files there."

Jake sat bolt upright in bed. "But of course you wouldn't have put the files there, would you, Trace?" He said these words aloud.

"I'm not following you."

You would never have risked giving me the decryption codes, would you? Jake's heart began to pound in his chest.

"That seems a reasonable conclusion. It would have been dangerous to make them so easily retrievable."

But you would have wanted me to find them, wouldn't you?

"Another reasonable conclusion."

Trace, what memories do you have of your creator's life?

"His life?"

Things unrelated to your work for the Trust, Jake explained, around the time when you worked on the chip.

"I remember having contact with Dr. Sarma, my grandfather, my sister, Trina. And you, of course."

Those are all related to your work in one way or another. I'm looking for something else. Something you did in your private life. Something that doesn't seem to have any significance, something... fun.

"Fun?" the Sim asked with a hint of irony.

I don't know. Things you did with friends or family, maybe?

"I had no friends outside of the Trust's sphere of influence, and my family was intimately involved in my work, especially Dr. Sarma. I enjoyed my research. I didn't have fun, as you put it."

What about hobbies? Movies? Vacations?

"I had little time for any of those things."

Why am I not surprised, Jake thought with a frown.

"I was quite dedicated to my work."

Great.

"What are you thinking?"

It's nothin'.

"In the ten years leading up to my death," the Sim said, "I did little other than work in the lab and travel to conferences in the field. Except, of course, for the sabbatical I took in Nepal to study—"

Sabbatical? In Nepal?

"Yes."

Why Nepal?

"I...," replied the Sim with uncharacteristic hesitation. *"I don't know what the purpose of the trip was."*

You have no recollection of what you did on the trip? None at all?

"None at all, although I assume the trip related to my study of meditative practices—control of heart rate and other bodily functions. The Nepali Buddhist monks are well schooled in such abilities."

Do you remember your other trips during that time?

"Yes, and in extraordinary detail."

Jake grinned.

"I take it you have your answer, then?" the Sim asked.

Yep. Looks like you'n I are goin' on a little trip, Trace.

JAKE peered into the Director's office the next morning.

"Come in, Jake," Haddon said. "You're here quite early."

"I think I may be onto something."

"Please have a seat and tell me what you're thinking."

"Thanks," said Jake, seated once more in front of Haddon's desk.

"I'm assuming this has something to do with Project Resurrection," the director prompted.

"Yes. It's not a sure bet, but it's something."

"Hmm." Haddon raised an eyebrow.

"Trace did some research in Nepal a few years before he began work on Project Resurrection," Jake began.

"Indeed, I seem to remember he spent nearly a year there."

"I've checked everywhere, and I can't find any information about why he took that trip," Jake continued. "Even the Sim has no record of what he did there, except that Trace made the trip."

"Interesting. And do you believe the encrypted files might contain information that relates to the trip?"

"I'm not sure. But I'm sure there is *something* about that trip that's relevant to the project and the files. A lead, maybe."

"I trust your instincts, Jake. It seems a logical place to begin your search for answers, in any event. Even if you don't find any clues to Trace's research or the computer files, it may be helpful to understanding Trace's state of mind."

"Thank you, sir," Jake said with relief.

"How long will you need?"

"Two weeks, give or take a few days."

"Then consider it a research assignment. And I'd prefer to keep this between us, for now," Haddon explained, "at least until we know more. I'd like you to keep me updated, of course."

"I'll check in from time to time and let you know how the work is progressing, sir," Jake reassured him.

"Good. Do you require any special equipment?"

"I don't think so. At least nothing I can't requisition myself."

"Then I look forward to your updates," said Haddon, standing up and smiling. "Good luck and safe travels."

Jake nodded, shook the director's hand, and walked out of the office.

chapter eight

In the Footsteps of Siddhartha

Life and death are one thread, the same line viewed from different sides.

—Lao Tzu

JAKE'S first stop in Kathmandu would be the Kopan Monastery, located in the great city. He discovered through Trina Michelson that Kopan hadn't been Trace's final destination but that he'd spent some time there studying. Through the monastery, Trace had made contact with the man with whom he had trained for the next eleven months: Khenpo Bokar Donyo.

After leaving his hotel first thing the next morning, Jake made a quick detour to the main market square for a disguise of sorts. In this society of understated dress and appearances, his crimson hair drew immediate attention. Preferring to keep a low profile, Jake stopped at one of the market stalls and purchased a locally made traditional woolen hat, then tucked his braided hair underneath.

While at the market, he noticed a number of other foreigners, not a surprise by any means—Kathmandu was popular as a tourist destination and a starting point for those seeking to train in the ancient Buddhist traditions of the region. Always keenly aware of his surroundings, he observed several university students from England haggling over woolen shawls, an elderly couple from the United States taking photographs, a group of middle-aged men seeking to engage a Sherpa to climb one of the nearby mountains, and a man about Jake's age with snow-white hair and blue eyes, who appeared to be shopping for souvenirs to bring back home. American, most likely.

From Kathmandu, Jake took a taxi to the base of Kopan Hill, which rose high above the terraced fields of the Kathmandu valley. From there, he climbed the hill to the monastery, a large conglomeration of brightly painted buildings, populated by monks dressed in traditional red robes. He smiled as he saw an English sign posted on the side of one of the buildings: "No killing, no stealing, no lying, no sexual conduct, no taking of mind-altering substances."

"Wise rules to live by," the Sim noted.

And not all so easy to obey, Jake replied.

It took Jake the better part of two hours to track down an elderly lama who spoke very little English, but who had known Bokar Donyo.

Jake spoke many languages fluently and without accent. Nepalese wasn't one of them. To his surprise, however, he soon learned that the Trace Sim *did* speak the local language. With the Sim's help, he was able to understand and respond to people he met in the town with little difficulty.

"It's interesting," the Sim said, *"that I remember nothing of this place, but I seem to be fluent in Nepalese."*

To Jake, this was just further proof that he was on the right track. He was convinced that the gaping hole in the Sim's memory wasn't a fluke; Trace had wanted him to discover it, and he had wanted him to come here seeking answers.

"I remember him," the old man told Jake in Nepalese, pleased to learn that Jake could understand him. "He taught here when the monastery was founded, but he left some time ago to return to his home village."

"Do you remember the name of his village?" Jake asked.

"He makes his home in the high foothills of the Himalayas. I believe he lives near Mirik."

Jake thanked the old monk and, upon his return to his hotel, used his computer to determine that Mirik was a small town located in the Darjeeling region of India and a popular tourist destination. There, he would attempt to discover the exact location of Trace's teacher, who was said to be living by himself in a small stone hut off the main roads.

JAKE spent nearly a week in Mirik searching for Khenpo Bokar Donyo, but to no avail. It was early on the seventh night that he decided upon a tiny restaurant located on the outskirts of the town for his dinner. Tired and hungry, he sat down at one of the few tables inside the ramshackle eatery and ordered a simple meal of dal bhat, a spicy soup made of lentils and served over boiled rice, with tarkari, a vegetable curry.

A young woman, no more than eighteen years old and dressed in a simple cotton sari, stopped by Jake's table as he ate. He recognized her as one of the cooks who had been working behind a curtain in the corner of the restaurant.

"I hear that you seek Khenpo Donyo," she said in Nepalese, not meeting Jake's eyes.

"Yes. I'm told I have much to learn from him—that he is a great khenpo."

"I am his great-niece. His brother was my grandfather."

"Then you know where he lives?" he asked, relieved to make some progress at last. "Can you take me to him?"

"I cannot take you to him," the girl answered. "My great-uncle passed on several years ago. He was very old."

This news was an enormous blow to Jake. "I didn't know that," he said, bowing his head out of respect. "I'm sorry I will not be able to meet him. I'd hoped to ask him about a friend of mine."

The girl smiled and looked down again. "Would you like to speak with my father? He spent many hours with the old man. Perhaps he can provide you with guidance in your studies. Our house is very near this restaurant—I can take you there now, if you wish."

"Thank you," said Jake. He put a few coins down on the table and stood up. "I'd like that."

They walked out of the restaurant and down a narrow, winding street that led toward the center of the town. After several minutes, they reached a tiny house with a crumbling white plaster façade. Several layers of paint were visible in spots, and bricks poked out from beneath.

"Come in," she said as she slipped off her shoes at the door. Jake did the same, ducking as he entered so as not to hit his head on the low doorway. Once inside, the girl led him into a small room, bare but for several cushions on the floor and a small altar covered with flowers and incense. "Please wait here. I will bring my father."

Jake bowed and sat cross-legged on one of the cushions. To say that he was disappointed to hear the old khenpo was dead was an understatement.

"Perhaps the nephew will be able to impart some information," the Sim offered hopefully. *"Perhaps I planned for just such an eventuality."*

I hope so, Jake replied, his frustration and fatigue threatening to get the best of him.

After a few minutes, a small middle-aged man entered the room, bowing formally to Jake. His dark hair was peppered with gray; his expression was one of genuine delight. Jake stood and bowed in return. "Namaste."

"Namaste. I am Ashish Donyo," the man said, gesturing for Jake to be seated.

"Thank you for allowing me to speak with you," Jake offered in Nepalese. "I'm Jake—Jacob Anders."

"Jacob Anders," repeated Ashish. "Would it be too much trouble for me to ask you to remove your hat?"

Jake wondered if he had committed some heretofore unknown social faux pas in wearing his hat inside the house. Ashish, perhaps sensing Jake's discomfort, smiled at him. "You have done nothing wrong, Jacob Anders," he explained. "I merely wish to confirm something."

Jake smiled back at the man with relief and pulled the woolen cap off his head to reveal his fiery red hair.

"Mr. Anders," said Ashish after a moment's pause, his face again lit with delight, "we have been waiting for you."

"Waiting… for *me*? I don't understand," a confounded Jake replied.

"My uncle and I have waited many years for your arrival."

"Waited for me?" Jake repeated.

"The Westerner with hair the color of fire," said Ashish, speaking the words as if they had been repeated many times before. "My uncle told me that you would come."

Jake said nothing; he didn't know how to respond.

Do you know anything about this? he asked the Sim.

"Nothing," Trace replied. *"Clearly, I didn't know you when I was last here."*

"My uncle has asked to speak with you." Ashish stood up and lit several sticks of incense.

"I'm sorry. I don't understand. I thought your uncle was dead."

Ashish merely smiled again. "He has asked that I guide you in meditation, Jacob Anders. There is something that he wishes you to learn."

He's nuts.

"I see no harm in meditation," the Sim replied. *"It's a skill you should practice more."*

Right.

"All right," Jake said. "I would appreciate your guidance."

"Very good," replied Ashish. "Please close your eyes, then."

The smell of incense in the room was now heady and thick. Jake became aware of how tired he felt, and his eyes closed at Ashish's suggestion.

Jake was competent at meditation practice, and it had saved his life in Union Station. Still, he'd never fully mastered the technique, and he'd never achieved the higher level of consciousness of which Trace had often spoken. There was no denying the focusing effect of the practice, nor the way in which he'd learned to relax his body, slow his heart rate, and increase or decrease blood flow as needed, but he was no convert, either, to the Buddhist tantric tradition.

This time, however, was different from all the times he'd meditated in the past. This time, it was as if his mind had freed itself from the present reality and reached beyond, to a place he'd never been before. He wondered vaguely if the incense was responsible for the drug-like state in which he found himself.

"Jacob."

He opened his eyes. He was no longer in the small house, in the room filled with incense. Instead, he was on a high mountain plain overlooking a valley far below. There were no trees here, but the grass beneath him was a blue-green color that seemed almost too vivid to be real. In the distance, thick clouds floated in a pale-blue sky. The air smelled fresh: mountain air, crisp and cool to his nostrils. He reached to touch the grass and felt the softness of the individual blades.

An old man sat cross-legged before him, still but for the breeze that moved a few folds of his *sanghati*, the traditional dark-red outer robe of Buddhist monks. His face was lined with age, but his eyes were the deepest shade of green Jake had ever seen. Much like the grass. Surreal.

"Who are you?" asked Jake, realizing that he wore a novice's white robes and that his hair hung loose over his shoulders.

"You know who I am," the old man replied with a meaningful smile.

"Bokar Donyo," Jake said, blinking in astonishment. "But you're...."

"Dead?" the old man offered. "I am what you might consider to be dead."

"I don't understand."

"Life is not the simple breakable line that you understand it to be. There is more than just a worldly existence—much more beyond that which you call 'being alive'."

Jake said nothing but gazed back out at the valley below. Thick clouds had moved in now, obscuring what lay beneath.

"But you have not come all this way to hear an old man speak of eternity, have you, Jacob?" There was a hint of lightheartedness in his words. Kindness as well. "You have come here seeking answers."

"I'm honestly not sure what it is I'm looking for," Jake explained. "I just know that you taught someone—a man who was important to me."

"Indeed," Bokar replied with a placid expression. "And it was he who told me you would come."

"*He* told you? You mean he came back here, after he met me…?"

"No, Jacob. He did not know you when he came here, and he never came back."

"But then how…?"

"How did he know you would come here if he had yet to meet you?" Bokar finished. "Just as life is not the simple progression of one thing to another, neither is time. Here, in this place between the living and the spirit world, time has little meaning."

Jake struggled to comprehend the old man's words.

"Trace knew that he was to meet you, Jacob," the old man explained. "It was what he saw here that led him to seek you out."

Bokar laughed softly to see Jake's skeptical reaction. "I realize that this is hard for you to understand, Jacob," he said. "But here, in this place, Trace had a vision of someone who would become 'important' to him, as you put it. Someone who would help him fulfill his wish to put right what had gone exceedingly wrong.

"Trace came here to search for many things," the ancient khenpo continued. "But the one thing he desired above all others was peace."

"Peace?"

"His soul was always tormented," explained Bokar, "always searching. I believe it was *you*, Jacob Anders, whom he sought."

"Me?" said Jake with a grim laugh. "How would I—"

"You, young Jacob, had much to offer him," Bokar interrupted. "You may still be able to guide him to his soul's rest, to show him the path to the next level of enlightenment."

"Then he's alive?" The thought left Jake nearly breathless.

"Alive?" Bokar repeated, appearing to consider the word. "That I do not know, being no longer of your world. But Trace Michelson had a strong will to live, and he was well schooled in the techniques of healing and renewal. He was an outstanding student."

"Techniques? What sort of techniques?"

"You know of these techniques. You have used them yourself, although you have yet to achieve the same mastery of them as your teacher."

Jake said nothing.

"I sense your lack of faith in your own abilities," the old man noted wryly. "Interesting, is it not, that Trace had faith in you where you do not?"

"Faith in me?"

"Precisely. He believed that you would surpass him. It is for this reason in part that he sought your help. But there was another reason, as well." Bokar looked at him, and he felt as though the man could sense his innermost thoughts.

"What was the other reason?"

"You must learn that for yourself" was all that Bokar would say.

Silence descended over them. After some time, Jake ventured, "Your nephew said there was something Trace wanted me to have—something you wanted me to know."

"Yes, indeed. It is something that Trace believed would help you on your journey."

"What is it?"

Bokar looked down at the ground between them. Where there was once grass, there now was a colorful sand mandala—the traditional tridimensional representation of the universe.

Jake remembered watching the monks create the sand paintings at the monastery in Kathmandu. The monks had spent days building the intricate geometric forms on the ground as the tourists watched, mesmerized.

"The mandala," the old man explained, "represents a combination of the enlightened mind and body of Buddha and is considered to have great power."

"But it's made of sand. I can't take it with me. How is this supposed to help me?"

Bokar nodded, his expression one of infinite patience. "It is true that the mandala is a fleeting thing. A strong wind blows, and it vanishes forever from existence. But it lives on in our hearts and minds, as it will live on in yours." He raised his hand and touched Jake gently on the forehead. "You will understand its value."

Jake looked down once more. The mandala was gone; the tiny colored grains of sand now swirled about, spinning and rising from the ground. Bokar too had begun to fade. Jake could see right through him to the clouds beyond. "But I don't understand the meaning of the mandala." The altered reality began to die away, and the drab room in Ashish's house came back into focus. "Is it a key to his research?"

"In time, Jacob, you will understand," he heard Bokar say from a great distance.

Jake blinked. It was Ashish who now smiled back at him.

I'm losing my mind, thought Jake. Had any of the conversation been real? Or had he imagined it all because he wanted so badly to speak to Bokar?

"You're not losing your mind," came the voice of the Sim. *"I experienced it as well."*

Like it helps to hear that from a voice inside my head, Jake grumbled, the irony not lost on him. *I'm probably imagining you too.*

"Hardly," replied the Sim.

"I have something that I wish to give to you," Ashish said, standing up and walking over to the makeshift altar. He opened a small lacquered box that sat nestled between the smoking incense there, and retrieved a faded photograph. He handed it to Jake.

"But this…," Jake began, looking at the photograph with growing wonder. "It's the mandala I saw."

"My uncle did not want you to leave empty-handed," Ashish said. "It is not the same as the original, but it will suffice for your purposes."

Haddon will want to see something tangible, thought Jake. *If there's something to be deciphered here….*

"It is not the same as the original, the one in your visual memory," Ashish repeated, "but it will suffice."

Jake had no idea what Ashish meant—to him, a tangible visible representation of the mandala from his otherworldly encounter with Bokar was far more valuable for his purposes than any visual memory. He would bring the photograph back to the lab and hope that it contained information that would help unlock at least some of the secrets of the Project Resurrection files.

JAKE took the first train back to Kathmandu the next morning and arrived back at his hotel later that afternoon. He still wasn't convinced that anything he'd seen in his meditative experience was "real" in any sense of the word, but instinct told him that he'd learned all he could about Trace's journey here more than a decade before.

The first flight out of Kathmandu didn't leave until the next day, and Jake spent nearly the entire time poring over the photograph of the mandala, with little success. Bleary-eyed and aching from bending over his computer, Jake called the hotel concierge and asked for a recommendation for a massage. Several minutes later, having gotten the name of a rejuvenation spa in an old monastery located several blocks from the hotel, Jake rode the elevator down to the lobby. Once more dressed in his Western clothing, he now wholeheartedly played the role of tourist.

Always aware of his surroundings, he glanced around the room. The usual smattering of tourists milled around the lobby, just returned from day-long jaunts or planning their evening entertainment. He scanned the rest of the crowd, pausing for a moment at the sight of a shock of white hair that peeked out from behind a newspaper—the same man he'd seen in the market several days before. Putting his hands into his pockets, Jake strode out of the hotel onto the square, crossed it, and headed toward the smaller side street on which the spa was located.

The air was cool and crisp, with a hint of frost, as was typical for this time of year. The city was full of people going about their business at the end of another day. Vendors lined the streets, selling various wares: tourist items, food and other necessities.

Jake stopped at a small cart and picked up a bit of bread and a small piece of fruit to quiet his growling stomach, then headed on toward his destination. He had almost reached the entrance when he realized that he was being followed—the white hair was unmistakable.

Anything in your database on this one? he asked the Sim as he continued to walk.

"American. Twenty-nine years old. Passport reads 'Samuel Klein'. Stated profession: electrical engineer. Travels often. Recently visited Chicago, Los Angeles, Bern, and Raleigh, North Carolina."

Raleigh, huh? Interesting.

"His home address is listed as Annapolis, Maryland."

Government, then, Jake mused. *Even more interesting.* He finished the last bit of bread and headed into the small storefront.

"Mr. Anders," greeted the woman behind the front desk. "The hotel called to say you would be coming over. Let me show you to the dressing room."

"Thank you," Jake replied with a smile. "I'm looking forward to this."

chapter nine

Mark, Tail, and Drop

Do not seek to follow in the footsteps of the men of old; seek what they sought.

—Basho

SPOTTING his mark in the crowd had been easy. Jake Anders was tall and broad shouldered, with long flame-red hair. *Hard to miss.* Sam Klein snorted under his breath. *Hell, it'd be easy to pick either* one *of us out in a crowd.* Lord knew he'd considered dyeing his own hair more than a few times.

Anders had apparently been thinking the same thing. Sam watched as Anders purchased a traditional hat from an elderly woman at the market. The old woman laughed and reached out to touch the American's crimson braid, running her withered fingers over it reverently and flashing him another smile. Anders then wrapped the braid around in a coil, placed the hat on his head, and bowed to her. She bowed back, and Anders quickly left.

Observing this interaction surprised Klein. It wasn't the fact that Anders chose to hide his hair that had surprised him, however. That was to be expected. No, what astonished Klein was that one of the Trust's best agents—one of the most efficient and deadliest assassins in the business—could be so gentle and kind toward a woman he'd never met.

When Sam had been given this assignment by his director, he'd been fully briefed on Jake Anders—his education, his fighting style, his weapons of choice. Sam was to make contact with the Trust's top ops man, although now wasn't yet the time. Anders was on an assignment, a quest of sorts by the looks of it, and Sam wanted to learn as much as he could about that mission. He had no intention of interfering with the other man's investigation before he discovered its purpose.

Time to look busy, he thought as he casually turned to examine the handmade merchandise of a vendor. He knew that Anders had spotted him, but he also knew he looked the part of a tourist picking out knickknacks for friends and family back home.

Anders entered the Kopan monastery. Taking advantage of the break, Sam went to a nearby market and purchased clothing so he could more easily blend in. If he was going to follow Anders outside the tourist areas without the Trust agent spotting him again, Sam knew that he would need to be less conspicuous. He purchased the inexpensive, drab clothing of a working-class Nepali, changed into it behind a building, and covered his hair just as Anders had done moments before.

Anders exited the monastery into the bright sunshine some time later, looked up and down the street, and headed north to the train station. Sam followed Anders onto a train headed for one of the smaller surrounding towns, boarding the train several cars back.

For several days, Sam followed Anders as he searched the tiny town of Mirik. Early on the seventh evening, he trailed his mark to a small eatery and waited with a few of the locals on a bench outside. From this vantage point, he could just barely see inside. Anders was speaking to a young woman. After a few minutes, Anders got up and followed the woman out onto the street.

Just my luck, thought Sam with a shake of his head. *I get to tail a ladies' man.*

He waited several blocks away, keeping an eye on Anders's destination from a distance. About two hours later, he reappeared.

Anders looked stunned—dazed, really—as he took the road that would lead him back to the train station. Sam continued to follow at a distance, and it soon became apparent that Anders had recovered whatever it was that he'd come to find. Sam guessed that Anders was likely to head back to the States on the next plane out, which left in two days.

They arrived back in Kathmandu just after midnight. The next afternoon Sam waited in the lobby, appearing to all the outside world to be reading the paper and listening to his iPhone. He was, in fact, monitoring calls being routed through the hotel's front desk. A beep came through the headphones, a signal that Anders had placed a call to the concierge. The Trust agent was looking for a massage, and the concierge recommended a spa not far from the hotel. The package he'd booked included a steam room, hot bath, and massage. He would be at the spa for at least three hours.

Sounds good to me. I can indulge a bit and then make contact.

His mark exited the elevator, looking the part of a man on vacation. Sam kept reading the paper without glancing up. As Anders left the hotel, Sam folded his paper, got up from the chair, and followed him out into the street, all the while maintaining a discreet distance. Once Anders was inside the spa, he waited a few minutes and then went in himself.

The spa was relatively small, but Sam figured that Anders wouldn't think much of seeing another tourist there. He followed the attendant to a room, where he disrobed. He thought it slightly odd that the attendant asked him to lie facedown first, but he dismissed it as simply a different custom in a different country.

He lay down on the table, pulled the sheet up to cover his bare ass, and closed his eyes. The sounds of soothing music filtered into the room, and he began to relax for the first time in nearly a week. He heard the door open and close and the sound of footsteps as the massage therapist walked into the room.

"Relaxed?" came a man's low voice.

"Hmm," he replied, disappointed that he hadn't been assigned a female therapist.

A strong arm clamped onto his neck, holding him down.

Crap.

He tried to turn around, but he couldn't move—a hard knee was now wedged into the small of his back.

Crap.

"Why are you following me, Klein?"

Double crap. He got the drop on me.

"I'm not following you," Sam responded with practiced calm. "I'm on vacation."

The pressure on his windpipe increased as Anders pressed his head harder into the face cradle, and he began to see stars.

"Wrong answer. Why are you following me?"

"I am *not* following you, you delusional bastard. I'm here on vacation."

This time Anders pushed down hard on Sam's back, yanking his head up by his white hair.

"Still not good enough."

"I was sent here to make contact with you," Sam croaked as he struggled to breathe. This wasn't exactly *how* he'd planned to make contact, but he wasn't willing to get his teeth kicked in over semantics.

"Who sent you?"

"CIA," he gasped.

"What section?" Anders demanded, letting up the pressure only enough that Sam could speak.

"Special ops. Biological."

"Who's your boss?"

"John Mitchell," he croaked.

"Why contact me, then? Why not go to Haddon? We're on the same side," Anders snapped, maintaining his hold on Sam's neck.

"No, we're not."

"Do you think I'm stupid? The Trust is a fucking deep-cover operation for the CIA."

"No, it's not… not anymore."

WHAT the hell is he talking about? Jake thought as he held the squirming man in his grip. He wasn't sure what he'd expected the guy to say, but this sure as hell wasn't it. *We're not CIA? Since when?*

"He speaks the truth," answered the Trace Sim.

He released his hold on the prone man, and Klein pushed himself up into a sitting position, then gasping for breath, rubbing his neck and ignoring the fact that the sheet had pooled on the table, leaving him fully exposed. Sam Klein barely reached Jake's shoulder. Without weapons, Jake knew he'd have little chance of getting out from under his grip. It was worth the risk to hear what the man had to say. That, and he was enjoying seeing his tail squirm.

"What do you mean, 'not anymore'?" he demanded.

And when the hell were you going to tell me this, Trace?

The Sim did not reply.

Klein glared at Anders and scowled as he rubbed his neck. "The split came after Trace Michelson was assassinated."

"Why didn't the government just come in and take over? Why let us think that we're all still government agents?"

"We've had agents in there, trying to figure out what was going on," Klein explained, looking irritated. "We couldn't risk destroying the Michelsons' work or the biotechnology that's still stored at the facility."

"You've had undercover agents in there? Working with us?"

"Yes. But most were neutralized." Klein spat out the last word, sounding bitter.

"Neutralized? No one's gone missing since I've been there," Jake retorted. "With the exception of three pieces of shit my team took care of a few months ago. And I can assure you they weren't working for your *friends*."

"You wouldn't have noticed, because they never went missing. They've just been neutralized."

"Explain."

"After Trace Michelson was killed, Haddon brought in a scientist who had been banned from the CIA for performing unapproved experiments on humans. Sick bastard."

"Synchack?"

Sam nodded. "Took his only daughter, Krista, and used her as his first test subject," he explained with a look of disgust. "Wiped her memory clean and 'reprogrammed' her. He wanted to control people, to create the ultimate agent who would follow orders, no questions asked."

"What does that have to do with the Trust? I haven't noticed anything strange. I guess Krista *is* a bit unusual, but it's not like she's an automaton."

Sam regarded Jake with an expression that bordered on pity. "How much time *do* you spend with the other people in the organization, Agent Anders?"

"Not much, I guess," he admitted. "I spend time with the people I work with in the lab and on assignment. Why do you ask?"

"Because my sister was one of the first of our agents to be neutralized."

"Your sister?"

Sam sneered. Then, ignoring Jake's question, he went on to explain, "After a certain amount of time, neutralized agents need to be reprogrammed again. A brain can only handle so much manipulation. Five times and the process turns agents into vegetables. Agents who end up like that are institutionalized."

Jake said nothing, not sure what to believe about Klein's description of the results of Synchack's research.

"The Trust is far more humane in its treatment of victims of experiments with illegal biotechnology than its own test subjects," Sam continued. "Although when Trace Michelson was running the show, it was different. Now the Trust has set its sights on a much more sophisticated and less invasive program to create elite agents. That's where Synchack comes in."

Jake had a bad feeling about what Sam was going to reveal next. He swallowed hard and asked, "What program are you talking about?"

"I'm talking about you, Agent Anders. And Project Resurrection."

How the hell does he know about Resurrection?

The Sim did not answer.

Damn good thing you're dead, Trace, or I'd strangle you myself!

"How do I know you're telling me the truth?" Jake demanded.

"You don't. But the CIA wants you as badly as the Trust wants to keep you. You have something valuable to both organizations."

Jake glowered at the naked man before him. "So what do you want from me?"

"I only came here to make contact with you. I'm supposed to give you a message."

"What message?"

"That my director wants to meet with you to discuss your future."

"I don't need to discuss my future with your director," Jake snapped. "I'm doing just fine where I am."

"If you believe that," Sam said with a shake of his head, "then I've overestimated your intelligence. Surely you must realize that Haddon and Synchack will kill you if they think it's in their best interests."

It's hard to argue with the truth.

"I have people watching me," he told Klein. "What do you have in mind?"

"In my wallet, there's a card for a repair service. Call that number, and a date and time will be arranged."

Jake got the card out of the wallet. "Repair-It-All Electrical Services?" He raised an eyebrow.

Klein chuckled. "I *am* an electrical engineer, after all, Agent Anders."

Jake walked to the door and paused, his hand on the doorknob.

"Something on your mind, Anders?" Klein asked with a sigh.

"Yeah," Jake replied. "I've got a question for you."

"Shoot," replied the other man.

"Who's your sister?"

Jake saw a muscle in Klein's jaw twitch. "Cathy Smyth," he replied. "Director Haddon's assistant."

chapter ten

Suspicious Minds

The absurd denial of the truth is natural to man.

—Swami Prajnanpad

JAKE boarded the plane the next day, having slept little the night before. He had, of course, assailed the Trace Sim with a barrage of questions, the answers to which had not been in the least bit satisfactory.

So you knew about the split but just decided not to tell me?

"*I only knew that in the event of my death, it was a distinct possibility.*"

If you knew, why the hell didn't you tell me?

There was no answer.

Dammit, Trace, you've been fucking keeping this from me! The least you can do is tell me what you know.

"*I am not programmed to reveal that information yet.*"

Yet? Yet? What the hell kind of answer is that?

"It's an honest answer," the Sim replied. *"My programming will not permit me to reveal anything more until you have acquired certain information."*

Information? Like what?

"I can't answer that. I don't know what that information is. I only know that when you obtain it, I'll be able to answer your questions. There's a trigger mechanism in my programming."

Now, sitting on the long flight back to the States, Jake felt as though he were going to explode with frustration.

"Your heart rate is elevated, Jake," the Sim told him.

Shut the fuck up.

Jake signaled the flight attendant for another drink.

Jake had flown on the same plane to Delhi as Klein, but they didn't sit near each other, nor did they speak again. Jake still wasn't sure if he should believe Klein's story, and he wasn't sure if he should trust the man, but there was no mistaking the danger that would come his way if the two of them were spotted chatting, even casually. Charles Haddon was intelligent and devious. Jake had little doubt that if the Trace Sim could identify Klein as a CIA agent, the director of the Trust could do so as well.

Of one other thing Jake was sure: he would speak to Klein's boss, John Mitchell, but he would wait until after the meeting before he decided what he would tell Haddon about it, if anything. Jake memorized the phone number on Klein's business card and then destroyed it. The whole proposition was risky. For all he knew, Mitchell and his group just wanted to get their hands on a Resurrection Sim. Jake would have to prepare for the meeting or he'd end up just as dead as if Synchack himself had done the deed.

A WEEK after Jake's return from Nepal, there still had been no word from Haddon or Synchack regarding the mandala or its possible use in decrypting the file provided by Tanvi. After scouring some more obscure texts at the university libraries around town, the Library of

Congress, the Internet, and even some of the Buddhist temples in the area, Jake had come up dry.

To get his mind off the mandala, he delved into his work on a joint research project with Greyson, who had returned from an assignment the day before. The project was one they had been working on together for over a year: DNA recognition for computer access.

"Protocols met?" Grey straightened up from an electron microscope that he'd been adjusting and looked over at Jake in anticipation.

"Protocols met," replied Jake as he watched Grey capture the data on the computer.

"Starting the third in the sequence. Ready?"

"Ready." Jake couldn't get the conversation with Klein out of his head. Was he really that out of touch? *I really wouldn't know if any of the Trust's agents were compromised.*

After a few minutes of silence, he asked, "What are you up to this weekend?"

"Nothing. You?"

"Nothing," Jake answered. How long had it been since he and Grey had done anything together—even a quick beer?

"Wanna ride this weekend?" Grey asked as he leaned back on his chair and kept an eye on the timer.

"Hell, yeah." Jake grinned and relaxed a little. He missed this, just shooting the breeze with Grey. It had been way too long. "I just got the Harley outta storage, and I've been dying to get it out on the road. Where are ya thinkin'?" He glanced back at the data on the screen.

"How about a trip to White Cloud?"

"Ride, then ferry over?"

Grey nodded.

"You got it," Jake said, looking up. "Is Trina coming along?"

"Nope. She has a 'girls' weekend' planned. Shopping, pedicures—that sort of crap."

"So this is a 'guys' weekend', then?"

"Why not?" Grey laughed. "No pedicures, though."

"Ya wouldn't see it under the boots, anyhow," Jake deadpanned. "What time you thinkin'?"

"First thing on Saturday morning—to beat the traffic—six, maybe? Work for you?"

Jake nodded. "Let's meet at my place. It's farther north and a better take-off point."

"We'll take your camping gear, then." Grey punched a few keys and scribbled something on his notepad.

THEY rode up to Manitowoc, Wisconsin, ferried over to Ludington, Michigan, then rode through the Manistee National Forest. It was about four in the afternoon when they made camp near White Cloud. Dinner was a simple affair: the fresh fish they had caught, grilled over the campfire.

"You're awful quiet," Grey said as he tossed a second beer at Jake.

"Just thinking." Jake popped the top of his beer and took a long draw on it. He'd been wanting to talk to Grey for months now, but now he wasn't sure what to say or even how to say it.

"Did you 'find' yourself in Nepal, or were you on a mission?"

"Both, sort of," Jake replied, enjoying Grey's discomfort and at the same time unwilling to reveal much about the trip. The Sim's words echoed in his mind: *"Trust no one, Jake."*

Grey took a deep breath, then chuckled awkwardly. "Damn, man. You're not going to make this easy, are you?"

"Is there a reason I should make *anything* easy for you?" Jake took another pull on his beer.

Grey frowned. "You've changed since you went to Nepal."

Jake knew exactly what Grey was getting at. "Changed how?" He avoided Grey's gaze, instead focusing on the now empty beer bottle.

"I'm not sure—I can't put my finger on it. You've just... changed."

"Yeah, I guess spiritual journeys'll do that." Jake tried to make it sound casual, without great success.

"Still having tea with your Sim?" Grey joked.

"We had a falling out, so no."

Grey appeared to decide upon a different approach. "Trina said you were acting strangely, that you were looking for information about a trip Trace took to Nepal."

"She told you to ask me about it, then?"

"Yeah," Grey admitted. "She's worried about you. I guess I am too. I mean, chasing halfway around the world after a dead guy—"

"He's *not* dead."

"We've been through this before." Grey shook his head in exasperation.

"He's not dead," Jake repeated adamantly. "I'm more sure of it now than I was before."

"But you saw his body—"

"Yeah, I know what I saw. I also know that he was the best damn agent the Trust has ever seen. Those techniques he taught us—to lower our heart rate, our breathing—he learned all that in Nepal."

"Man, you're damn stubborn, aren't you?"

"He wants me to find him."

"Like hell," growled Grey. "I'm beginning to wonder if that Sim isn't making you nuts."

"Believe what you like. I'm perfectly sane."

"Perfectly delusional, you mean."

For a few minutes there was uncomfortable silence, interrupted at last by Jake's cell phone. The display on the phone read "060." He recognized the code, and his brow knitted in surprise. He tapped the phone.

"Director Haddon, what can I do for you?"

Grey raised a questioning eyebrow.

"Yes, Grey's with me," Jake responded after a pause. "We're camping in Michigan, 'bout five hours away."

"What does he want?" Grey mouthed.

Jake shrugged and shook his head, then said into the phone, "When? Of course—we'll be there. Good night, sir."

Jake tapped the phone to end the call. "He wants us for a mission. We're supposed to meet in his office at two tomorrow afternoon."

"*Both* of us? On a *Sunday*? What the fuck's going on, Jake?"

"No clue. But we'd better get some sleep. We'll need to leave by seven if we're going to make it back in time." Jake was silently relieved at having an excuse not to continue the conversation. The entire situation seemed to get stranger by the minute, and he had no doubt whatsoever that this new development had everything to do with the Trace Sim and Project Resurrection. He was getting nervous. *Really* nervous. And he still hadn't asked Grey about the Ares Sim.

THE next day found the two agents seated in the director's office, waiting to be briefed. "I'm sorry to cut your weekend short, gentlemen, but I need you both for this mission."

"No problem, sir," said Grey, all business.

"I've asked you to come here because I've received word of a disturbing development at a lab in Switzerland," Haddon explained as he picked up a file folder on his desk and opened it.

"Switzerland?" Jake asked.

"Bern, to be precise," Haddon replied. "Seems as though a Swiss research group has been using technology surprisingly similar to that upon which Project Resurrection is based."

"Resurrection?" Jake said with surprise.

"Indeed," replied Haddon. "Agent Lane has been briefed about your work to date on retrieving Trace Michelson's data. Since you two are the only recipients of Trace's modified chips, I thought I'd pair you up this time."

So Grey knew what's been going on, but he didn't say anything? What the hell game is he playing? His next thought was of Sam Klein, who had recently traveled to Bern.

"Of course, sir," Jake replied, his face impassive despite his anger.

"Lane's nanotechnology expertise will also be invaluable to this mission," Haddon continued. Then, picking up two packets and handing one to each of the men, he explained, "Your mission will be to retrieve whatever technology the Swiss firm has developed and eliminate any residue, as needed. The mitigation team will be on standby, awaiting your signal."

From "residue," Jake understood that this was a cleanup job as well. Remediation and, if necessary, termination of test subjects. Despite his anger, Jake was secretly relieved to have Grey's company on this type of mission—trained assassin or not, he didn't enjoy killing.

"WHEN the fuck did Haddon brief you on my work?" Jake demanded in a low, menacing voice as they sat side by side on the flight from Chicago to Munich a few hours later. Here, at least, Jake was pretty sure they'd not be overheard by Haddon's "ears."

Unless, of course, Grey is one of them. The thought was unsettling.

"A few days after you got back from Nepal."

"When the *hell* were you going to tell me?"

"I had a feeling the boss'd be asking us to go on some wild goose chase" was Grey's even reply. "I thought I'd wait until then."

"Who else knows?" Jake demanded.

"No one you don't already know about: Synchack, Krista, Dr. Carroll."

"And Trina?"

"She suspects something's up. She's sharp. Besides, you've been pretty obvious with your questions."

Jake took a deep breath and looked around the cabin. *How much do I tell him?*

"Trace trusted him," came the voice of the Sim. In his anger, Jake had nearly forgotten about the chip. *"Although I know nothing more than you do about what has transpired since my creator's death."*

He'd keep it brief, then—hedge his bets. If what Klein had told him was true, any Trust agent could be compromised, even Lane. Whatever he said needed to be something he was willing to reveal to Haddon himself.

"The Trace Sim is programmed not to reveal any more information regarding Project Resurrection until I've decrypted the Thebes files," he offered. Safe enough territory.

"And you're thinking the key to decrypting them is in the photograph you brought back?"

"Maybe. But Synchack hasn't been able to get anywhere with it yet. He was talking about consulting with some of the crypto guys to see if there's a hidden code in the design, last I heard."

"Sounds like a good start."

"Even if they find something in the design, though, I don't think that'll unlock the files. Trace was too smart for that. Dead or alive, he'd have anticipated that others would try to get their hands on the research. He'd have wanted to make this difficult."

"I agree." Grey ran his hand over the cup on the tray table in front of him. Coke.

Jake was reminded of the first time he'd met Grey, back in college.

"There's something else you should know," Jake said, deciding that he would risk revealing a bit more. In spite of his distrust of Charles Haddon, he couldn't shake the instinct to trust Greyson.

The other man looked at him inquisitively but said nothing.

"When I was in Nepal, I spotted another agent. Government guy. He tailed me," Jake explained. "The Sim ID'd him as CIA. I'm not sure how much he knows about Resurrection, but he's been traveling to some of the same places I have."

"Really? Why have one of our own tail you?"

"Dunno," said Jake. "But he's been in too many of the same places for it to be a coincidence. He was in Bern four weeks ago. Before that, he was in North Carolina."

"You think another group picked up Trace's research?"

"Probably."

"This is gonna be fun, then," said Grey as an impish grin spread across his face. "Lots of fun."

THE sun was barely up when they arrived in Switzerland the next morning. Their mission was a relatively simple one: infiltrate the small privately owned research facility at the edge of the city, recover whatever information might be stored in the computer database there, destroy the evidence, and leave whatever victims of experimentation they might find for the mitigation team.

Jake and Greyson had gone over the plan during the flight using their notebooks. Having pulled up the schematics of the building on the devices and noted the access points, they would go in as HVAC environmental specialists.

The pair made their way to the facility in a service vehicle and parked by the receiving and maintenance entrance at the rear of the building. After syncing their watches, they exited the van and retrieved their tools, then slipped on their white environmental suits, leaving off the attached hoods and masks.

Grey stepped up to the security sign-in booth and introduced himself to the guard.

"You're not the usual crew," the man observed, looking Jake over as he signed the log sheet.

"This is a persistent problem, so they called us in to fix it once and for all," Jake answered in flawless Swiss German.

The guard nodded in answer, handed them access badges, and called for the maintenance head to come show them to the room where the HVAC unit was located. While Jake distracted the guard with conversation, Grey reached under the counter and planted a jamming device, which would be activated when the time was right.

The head of maintenance, a burly man who reeked of stale cigarettes, explained the problem with the lack of air circulation, foul odor, and temperature control, showing them several pages of notes from the earlier repair crew. The earlier HVAC crew had been a fake, of course—local Trust operatives who had created the cooling problem during a routine maintenance visit to the facility. The temperature in the facility was now easily twenty-nine degrees centigrade.

"We'll need to take air readings in the entire building. Some areas may need to be evacuated," Jake explained to one of the other employees as he wiped sweat off his brow.

"I understand. Let me know if you need anything," the man replied, leaving Grey and Jake alone to begin their testing.

Grey and Jake pulled out their notebooks. "I'll meet you here." Grey pointed to a spot on the diagram. "Thirty minutes. I'll start jamming in fifteen."

The two men slipped the white hoods over their heads and donned their breathing masks. They parted without further discussion, headed down opposing hallways.

GREY switched his notebook to the security camera feeds and watched Jake disappear down another hallway on the screen. When Jake was well out of earshot, Grey pulled his mask and hood off, took his phone out of his pocket, and tapped it twice. "I'm in," he said. "You've got ten minutes, max, before Anders reaches it." He hurriedly repocketed the phone and continued on to his destination, a room near the innermost part of the building.

JAKE made his way to the DNA lab and the storage room beyond it. From the information the Trust had gathered, the lab had recently perfected the process of storing electronic information on a new medium, producing a quarter-sized wafer-thin disk that could hold a thousand times more data than its predecessor.

As he rounded the corner to the corridor where the lab was housed, Jake looked up to see a security camera pan around to focus on him. He extended the telescoping pole that took air samples and pretended to jot down a reading on his smart phone.

Grey should have the cameras on bypass by now.

He heard a faint *click* of a bolt and a female researcher exited the DNA lab, passed him quickly, and disappeared down another hallway. Before the door could close, Jake was able to slip inside without having to disable the key reader. *That was lucky.*

The lab was completely empty. There were no researchers, no test subjects—nothing.

Odd. Core work hours, and no one is here? Not good. He turned the corner to see the door to the storage room wide open. The area around the lock was blackened.

Explosives. Shit. Someone else got here first.

On one of the high tables, Jake spotted a special stand that he knew held the wafers. The stand, which appeared to have storage for three wafers, now only held two. Jake spoke into the tiny microphone on his uniform. "Grey, we've been compromised. Looks like someone made off with one of the wafers."

There was no response.

"Grey?"

Shit. What was going on? He quickly grabbed the remaining wafers off the stand and placed them in a case on his belt. He slipped two earplugs out of his pocket and placed them in his ears, then ran out of the storage room and was just about to slip back into the hallway when the fire alarm sounded—Grey, creating a diversion so that Jake could locate possible test subjects.

A voice came over the loudspeakers in English. "Please exit the building in an orderly fashion. This is only a drill...." The voice repeated the warning in German, Italian, and French.

Jake checked all the rooms that could possibly hold test subjects; each time, he came up dry. The alarm silenced as he finally made it to the last lab. He pointed his cell phone at the keypad, and the door clicked and slid open. The lab appeared to have been ransacked. Jake drew his gun.

I'm really not liking this.... He saw streaks of blood on the wall, splatters all over the computer monitors, and three bodies on the floor—each lying in a small pool of blood.

Shit!

"Grey!" Jake shouted into his microphone. "Get the hell out of there!"

He heard footsteps in the hallway and ran outside the lab, gun pointed in front of him. Gunshots echoed from nearby—someone was firing into the corridor. He hit the floor and rolled just as the light above him exploded, showering glass in a thousand different directions. He got to his feet and moved quickly. He ducked around the next corner, running his hand against the wall to find his way in the pitch blackness.

Fucking shit! We've been set up. How the hell did they know we'd be here?

"Jake, there's an emergency exit two feet to your right," said the Trace Sim.

Jake threw down a smoke pellet and pushed through the door. As he exited into the bright sunshine, a cloud of black smoke billowed behind him and rose up into the sky. One of the mitigation team members posing as part of the local rescue squad escorted him away from the building and back to the van he'd arrived in less than an hour before. Grey was already standing by the van. They climbed inside and drove off.

"What the fuck happened back there?" demanded Jake. "And why the hell didn't you respond?"

"I ran into some trouble. The com lines were jammed. Seems someone got here before we did."

"Yeah, I figured as much, what with the storage room lock blown and one wafer missing. There were three dead bodies in one of the other labs."

"One wafer was missing?"

"Yeah, why?"

"The bitch who shot at me took the other wafer."

Jake looked at him. "A woman? Brunette, hair up in a clip, glasses, navy pants, white shirt, white lab coat?"

"Yeah, why?"

"She came out of the lab just before I went in," Jake answered, frustrated. "Did she get away?"

"No—I took her down and retrieved the other wafer."

"Who was she?" Jake peeled his suit off as Grey continued to drive.

"No idea."

"The agent in question is a highly qualified researcher within the National Institutes of Health," the Trace Sim supplied.

Great, another government agent.

"I don't like this. Whole damn thing was a setup. What the hell were the feds doing here?"

"What?" Grey choked, shock apparent on his face. "How do you know they were government?"

"The Sim identified her. Government. NIH researcher."

"Shit."

"Yeah, that just about sums it up." Jake scowled and shook his head.

What the hell is going on here?

"It seems someone anticipated your arrival," the Sim offered. *"A leak, perhaps?"*

Shit. Shit, shit, shit.

LESS than twenty-four hours later, Grey and Jake waited in Haddon's office for debriefing. Haddon, apparently as unperturbed as ever, sat down and glanced at the paperwork his assistant had left on his desk.

For several minutes he said nothing. Then, raising his eyebrows and smiling, he closed the file folder and looked up at the two men.

"Gentlemen, it appears the wafers you secured are the key to decrypting the first of the Project Resurrection files obtained in Raleigh. Congratulations on a mission well done."

Jake and Grey looked at each other with palpable relief.

"Now for the troubling part." Haddon took off his glasses and rubbed his forehead. He sighed, then put his glasses back on before continuing, "The agent you ran into at the site was part of a CIA deep ops group. A sister organization, of sorts. It appears the group has gone rogue."

This is fucking surreal, Jake thought, doing his best not to betray his shock.

Haddon added, "Grey, you may remember the leader of this operation—one of Trace's mentors."

"Sir?" Grey looked equally puzzled at the news.

"John Mitchell, head of the CIA's Avadhuta Group."

"The plot thickens," the Trace Sim added sardonically.

chapter eleven

Crash and Burn, Baby

As long as you seek for something, you will get the shadow of reality and not reality itself.

—Shunryu Suzuki

FUCK. Shit. Damn.

Jake repeated these words in his mind like a twisted mantra all the way back to his apartment. He and Grey hadn't spoken after the debriefing with Haddon, Grey having mumbled something like, "I haven't seen Trina in days, so why the fuck would I want to have a few beers with you?" before hopping into his own car without any further ado.

Jake turned the key in the lock, closed the door behind him, and tossed his shirt and shoes onto the floor before grabbing a beer and settling into his favorite chair.

Shit, shit, shit. This is bad.

And what was even worse than the jumbled thoughts bouncing around his brain was the nagging feeling in the back of his mind that he'd missed something—a clue, perhaps—something he should have considered. There was something wrong here, something *very* wrong. He just wasn't seeing the big picture. He pulled his cell out of his pants pocket and tapped ten numbers quickly into it.

"Repair-It-All Electrical Services." A woman's voice. Professional and entirely unremarkable.

"Name's Jake Anders," he said in a clipped tone. "I need to schedule an appointment. This week. Earliest available."

"Just a moment, Mr. Anders. Let me pull up the schedule." There was a brief pause, and then, "How would tomorrow afternoon at two o'clock work for you?"

"That'd be fine."

"Thank you for calling Repair-It-All, Mr. Anders," the woman told him. "Please feel free to call us if you need to reschedule."

"Will do. Thanks." He disconnected the call and tossed the phone onto the coffee table.

Where is Mitchell's office? he asked the Sim, taking a long drink from his beer.

"Midway between DC and Annapolis," came the reply.

Jake set the alarm on his phone for 2:00 a.m., then finished his beer and lay back on the couch. The trip by car would take him nearly twelve hours. He wouldn't risk flying—the Trust monitored its agents' movements too closely for that. That would give him nearly eight hours to rest before the drive. He closed his eyes.

Ten minutes later, he stood up and walked around the apartment, stretching. He began to pace, back and forth.

Why am I not seeing this?

"You're tense, Jake."

Damn Sim. He hadn't had a conversation with it since Nepal, at least nothing more than the technical advice he'd needed for the Swiss job. Still, much as he was loath to admit it, he found that he missed the tea and conversation Grey had mercilessly teased him about.

The Sim was right, though—he needed to rest. He'd need to be thinking clearly for the meeting with Mitchell. He lay back down on the couch.

"Relax, Jake. Let me guide you in meditation."

He wanted to pull the damn thing out of his head. He was getting tired of all the unanswered questions, of all the evasive responses. He wanted… something. Something more than this limbo in which he found himself—this not knowing.

"Close your eyes, Jake, and imagine a restful place—a place where you'll be undisturbed."

He took a few breaths and grumbled, "Okay."

He closed his eyes and imagined himself on a beach overlooking blue-green water. He could hear the sound of the surf hitting the sand; he felt the spray on his face and the warmth of the sun. He took a deep breath and followed the Sim's instructions.

HE FELT a strong pair of hands on his chest and shoulders, digging into the tense muscles there from above him, kneading at the stiffness. The surf pounded the shore, and a drop of salt water hit his cheek. For the first time during a meditation, he realized he could *smell*—the tangy scent of seaweed washed up on the sand, the salt on the breeze, and something else—the citrus aftershave he remembered from years before. Trace's aftershave. It was deeply unnerving. It was as though Trace were there with him, beside him. The real Trace and not a simulation. He fought the urge to stand up and start pacing again.

"Relax." Trace Michelson's resonant voice was a surprising balm for the stress Jake could not seem to release. The voice was also different than before: warmer, perhaps. No longer in his mind, but right there, next to him. Real. Much like the difference between a painting of a beautiful sunset and the sunset as it paints the world with vibrant color, because you are there to experience it.

"You've never touched me before." Jake marveled at the strength in those long, graceful fingers. He could almost hear the other man's breath in his ear as he imagined Trace's face above his own, looking down. He didn't open his eyes for fear that the scene would disappear and he'd be back in his own apartment once more, alone.

"You've never *let* me touch you, not in this way," the Sim responded. "Until now, you haven't been comfortable letting me get this close to you."

"Hell." Jake sighed and gave in to the need to believe that it was Trace Michelson touching him, and not just a simulation. "It's all in my head, anyhow. Why should I care what you do?" He began to relax into the warm sand, and all thoughts of what Grey might say if he told him his Sim massaged his shoulders on a Caribbean beach vanished.

"You will find the answers." Trace began to work his way down Jake's arm, kneading the muscles. "But you must be patient."

"Easy for you to say," said Jake with a laugh. Trace worked his fingers up Jake's arms and lingered briefly at his shoulders, working through the tension, reaching around his neck to work the muscles of his upper back. Painful bliss.

"Relax," Trace commanded after a few more minutes. Jake obliged as his head sank back further into the soft sand.

"God, that feels so good."

"You're fighting it," Trace said, his face again close to Jake's.

"Hell no. It's just that I'm starting to feel like Jell-O."

"I'm not talking about your body," the Sim replied. "I'm talking about your mind, your spirit."

"My mind?"

"You must open your mind, Jake, and see the infinite possibilities."

A flash of color hovered on the periphery of Jake's consciousness: the mandala. "What am I supposed to see in it?" he asked as Trace caressed his chest. "What am I missing?"

"The future. Your future is there."

"Right now, I'm just seein' myself dead," Jake answered acerbically. "And that's what I see, no matter which way I look."

"You're better than that—stronger. You're capable of so much more than you're willing to admit. This is no different from any mission you've been sent on in the past. Only perhaps there is more to be gained in the end."

"Will you be waiting there?" Jake asked.

There was no answer. Trace followed a line to the sensitive skin under Jake's ear, and Jake felt gooseflesh rise on his body.

"God, Trace," he whispered, "what are you doing?"

"I'm merely responding to your wishes, to your desires." Jake imagined Trace's lips close to his ear. "It's what I'm programmed to do."

"My... desires?" Jake wondered aloud. "Trace... he programmed you to...?"

"My programming has never been completely static," Trace replied as he ghosted a pair of silken palms over the muscles of Jake's chest, and Jake's body arched instinctively upward. "I'm only responding to your needs, your desires."

"Have I desired this?" Jake mused. He was a sexual being, although he'd never found a man who could completely satisfy him. And yet, this man whom he'd worshipped from afar....

"You hesitate because you do not know what to believe of your unspoken need," Trace explained calmly.

"I...."

"It's your desire that guides me. And it's your fear that holds you back."

"I'm afraid," Jake admitted.

"You're afraid of being with me." Jake knew Trace was right. Was it so unreasonable to be afraid of Trace? He was nothing more than a ghost.

"How did you know," Jake asked, uncomprehending, "when I didn't understand it myself?"

"I'm a part of you. I can't be separated from you, nor can I fail to hear what's in your heart."

Jake moaned again. The feel of Trace's fingers on his scalp made him want to....

"Open your eyes, Jake Anders," that glorious voice now commanded. "Open your eyes."

Jake obeyed, looking into the most stunning eyes he'd ever known, their deep blue now appearing almost gray in the bright sunlight. It was as if he were seeing those eyes for the first time—they were no longer the cold, controlled eyes of the man who had mentored him but the eyes of a lover, warm and deep. Trace was naked, his hair wet from the water. Jake realized that he was naked, as well.

"Trace," he whispered as their lips met. He ran his fingers over the well-defined chest, the smooth pale skin that seemed to glow in the sunlight. "You're so goddamn beautiful. I never knew…." His voice trailed off as he felt Trace run his hands through his hair with its ends now painted in sand. Trace licked his ear, and Jake gasped. Why did this all seem so real? And how hadn't he understood what he'd felt all along? He smiled for a moment at the realization that Grey had correctly guessed at his heart, then silently cursed the man for it.

"Do you understand, now, what you've denied yourself all these years?" Trace whispered, biting the lobe of Jake's ear and sucking it for a moment. "Do you understand why I always kept you at arm's length?"

"You didn't want to hurt me." Jake was momentarily stricken by the thought that the real man behind the Sim might not have desired him in the same way. To Trace, he'd been just a kid, eager, willing, and yet unable to comprehend the adult whispers of his soul.

Jake couldn't deny it any longer: after years spent with the Sim as his constant companion, he'd grown to love Trace. It was utterly absurd. But as he lay on the beach with the water lapping at his toes, the absurdity of falling in love with the ghost who inhabited his mind didn't matter. Here, in this place, that love felt real.

"I wanted you to make your own choices."

I want this now. I want him.

Jake pulled Trace on top of him, raking his back with his nails until he heard a low groan in response. Then, roughly, he drew Trace's face back to his and found his lips once again, probing Trace's mouth with an insistent and demanding tongue, relishing the warmth as it opened to him. He had never tasted anything as sinfully sweet.

"Jake, what do you want?" Trace wrapped his arms around Jake and pulled him closer.

"I want *you*," moaned Jake, his hands grasping at the tensed muscles of Trace's shoulders, feeling the power there.

Trace pushed Jake back onto the sand, his eyes hooded with lust. He sucked hard at the base of Jake's neck, then moved lower, biting a nipple and laving the outline of it with his tongue. Jake growled as Trace took the pebbled flesh between his teeth and rolled it there, biting it again, just enough to sting.

"Oh, fuck… Trace!" he cried out. Where did a Sim chip learn to do that? The thought was quickly replaced by thrumming need. He went to push Trace over, to dominate him as he was being dominated, but Trace was far stronger than he remembered, and he remained pinned beneath the smaller man.

Trace's eyes grew darker still as he pushed Jake's wrists into the sand at his sides. Jake ceased his struggle, surrendering to his companion until he felt Trace's hard cock against his. But the blissful pressure of that contact was quickly gone as Trace leaned down, then drew lazy circles on his abdomen with his pink tongue, making his way slowly downward to the point that Jake thought he might lose his sanity in the pleasure of the other man's touch.

"God, Trace." The sun-heated water lapped at Jake's feet as Trace's lips parted and he felt the warmth of Trace's mouth, exploring the length of him, tasting and sucking there.

Now I've really lost my mind.

"Hardly," murmured Trace, circling his tongue around the sensitive tip before swallowing it down until his mouth met the reddish curls at the base of Jake's cock. "You've just found it."

He could barely breathe to feel that warm heat. And that tongue! God, that tongue was at once both heavenly and sinful. Trace sucked in his cheeks, increasing the pressure—that incredible, perfect pressure that made Jake forget everything. Teeth, lips, and tongue combined in the most exquisite way.

Jake realized his lover no longer held his wrists when he felt lithe fingers scrape the sensitive skin of his perineum and a firm hand cup his balls, then roll them about. "Shit!" he cried out, the sound of his voice lost on the crashing waves. "Shit, shit, shit!" A finger pressed against his tight opening, and it was just too much for him. He came hard in Trace's mouth, shuddering and clutching Trace's hair in his hands.

THE cell phone alarm buzzed, and Jake awoke with a start, panting. He was still on the couch, wearing the same pair of pants as before. The apartment was dark. He was soaked in sweat. He felt the sticky warmth of his release on his abdomen. He was half-hard just remembering.

"Helluva dream," he muttered to himself. He got up and headed for the shower, stripped off his pants, and set the temperature as cold as he could stand it. "You are one fucked-up SOB," he added, shaking his head and grabbing the shampoo.

That was a dream, wasn't it? he wondered as he rinsed the shampoo from his long hair.

The Sim remained silent.

chapter twelve

Knocking on Heaven's Door

Knowledge overcomes ignorance as sunlight darkness.

—Atmabodha Prakasika

CHARLES HADDON tapped a button on his desk, and within seconds, Cathy Smyth walked into the room.

"What can I do for you, sir?"

"I'd love a pot of tea," Haddon replied, returning her blank smile. "Black this time, not green."

"Of course, sir." She scurried out of the office.

Haddon opened his personal notebook and perused the information on the screen with renewed interest. He'd read the report several times before—Trace's notes, or at least part of them, finally decrypted:

Psychotropic Effects of Initial Sim Protocol:

Stage One: Of the initial six volunteer subjects, four showed signs of altered reality and hallucinations, becoming paranoid and delusional. Upon removal of chip, only two showed signs of improvement and ultimately recovered. Of the two remaining test subjects affected, neither responded to removal or drug therapy, and both were subsequently euthanized. The protocol was terminated.

Stage Two: Six volunteer subjects were injected with an anti-anxiety drug before implantation. Two of the six subjects still experienced the same psychotropic effects of the initial study group. Dosage of anti-anxiety drug was increased. Only one of the test subjects reacted favorably. One subject did not improve and was subsequently euthanized. The protocol was terminated.

DNA analysis of the test subjects revealed a particular pairing of genes predisposed certain individuals to the psychotropic effects. Continued testing and analysis indicated that a series of injections with a drug and vitamin combination every three weeks for six months prior to chip implantation was successful in preventing the psychotropic effects of the chip.

Stage Three: Thirty-six subjects tested after receiving vaccination. Only one showed slight psychotropic symptoms. Upon removal of the chip, symptoms abated.

"Sir?" Haddon looked up to see Cathy reenter the office with a tray in her hands. They were trembling slightly, causing the delicate china tea set to ring.

"Please, Cathy," Haddon said kindly, "put the tray down and tell me what's on your mind."

"We have a situation, sir," she almost squeaked. Her round face was pale, and she was visibly shaken. She didn't look at him; her eyes focused fixedly on a bookshelf over his shoulder. "The latest security scan indicates our servers have been breached and that data is being sent to another location."

"Have we located the source of the breach?"

"Dr. Synchack believes that the breach may have originated with the wafers Agents Lane and Anders retrieved in Bern."

"Is Agent Lane still compliant?"

"Yes, sir. Dr. Synchack does not believe another neutralization is necessary at this time."

"I see. Thank you, Cathy. Please inform Vasalia that I'll speak with him shortly. I'll buzz you if I need you."

Cathy walked back out of the office, looking relieved.

Haddon glanced back down at Trace's notes and scanned the pages of electronic data until a single name caught his eye: Jacob Anders. He ran his long fingers over the print, reading down to see what more information, if any, he could glean from the notations.

So Anders has the DNA patterns associated with the psychotropic reactions in the test subjects. Interesting.

He paused for a moment, mulling over the significance of this additional information. Anders had already shown some mental instability, as evidenced by his behavior in Union Station and his obsessive pursuit of anything related to Trace Michelson. The documentation demonstrated that implantation of the chip inside a host with a similar DNA configuration would lead to complete deterioration of the host's mental faculties within a sixty-month period.

He's losing his mind, mused Haddon. *And there's nothing anyone can do about it.*

Haddon picked up his phone and punched in a three-digit extension. "Agent Lane," he said, "I have a job for you."

THE weather in the Washington area was hot and humid, as to be expected of late summer. Jake, having run several quick tests on his Audi S roadster to be sure that no tracking devices had been planted on it in his absence, revved the engine as he wove in and out of the heavy DC traffic. He had left his company-issued cell phone and watch at the apartment. Haddon wouldn't be able to track his whereabouts, at least not easily.

He was far too keyed up to be tired from the long drive; in fact, the trip had done him a world of good. That and the dream that he couldn't help but recall as the road stretched out before him. At least he now had the answer to one more question amongst the myriad questions that remained.

"The entrance is on the side," the Trace Sim told him. *"No doubt they're expecting you."*

I'm just supposed to walk in there?

"And why not?"

Haddon already thinks I'm holding something back. What if he has this place watched?

"There is no other option at this point—you've already chosen your course."

Small consolation when I'm looking at a bullet to the brain.

He parked his car, set the alarm, and headed into the unexceptional office building. From all outward appearances, the Avadhuta Group was just another nondescript government agency, filled with nondescript men and women pushing paper and accomplishing little, but still managing to waste taxpayer money. The reception area was replete with standard government-issue furniture and painted a drab, yellowing white. Photographs of the President and the Vice President hung on the walls.

Jake flashed a charming smile at the receptionist, an attractive woman with long auburn hair and blue eyes. "Jake Anders. I have a two o'clock appointment."

She looked him over with obvious interest and said, "Of course, Mr. Anders. The director is expecting you." She pressed a button on the desk, then walked out from behind it to shake his hand. "I'm Lottie Grier. I'll be your escort around the facilities."

Within moments, another woman had appeared to take her place behind the counter, and Lottie looked relieved. "I've never learned to use the damn phones." She rolled her eyes as she motioned him through a set of double doors and into a long hallway.

"You're not the receptionist?" He'd already guessed, of course, but he figured it wouldn't hurt to ask.

"No, of course not," she said with a musical laugh. "I'm with the Director's Office. Security."

Security? Damn good-looking security.

"She is quite lethal," the Sim offered. There was a hint of irritation in its voice.

Lottie guided him into a small sterile-looking room and shut the door behind them. "Weapons?" she asked.

Jake reached under his jacket and pulled out his Walther PPK handgun. She took it without comment and set it on a small table in the center of the room, then waited. His eyes met hers, and after a pause he pulled a small knife from his belt. She took this from him as well, then smiled patiently at him.

"Anything else?"

"No," he lied.

She laughed, then unexpectedly pulled him toward her and kissed him on the lips, her hands tracing the hard muscle of his torso beneath his jacket.

"What the hell…?"

"A girl's gotta have a little fun, right?" she trilled, twirling a second knife around in her fingers. She had pulled it out from the back of his pants.

He frowned. "Done yet?"

"Not quite." She batted her eyelashes at him, bent down so that her head was set provocatively at the level of his groin, then laughed once more and stood up, holding the tiny dagger he wore strapped to his shin, right above the ankle.

"I'm impressed." And he *was*. He offered her a sheepish grin.

"You shouldn't be," she sighed. "I'm too much of a lady to get the last one myself. Would you mind?"

He snorted and shook his head, then reached into his pants pocket and down his pant leg to pull out his favorite knife—the one he'd owned since before he'd come to work for the Trust.

"It was tempting," she admitted, placing the last knife on the table and pointing toward the door at the back of the room. "You're a nice-looking man, you know." This last sentence was purred.

They walked out the door and down another corridor. She withdrew a lanyard from inside her shirt—it had been wedged into her cleavage—and swiped a card through the reader by the next set of doors, which opened automatically with a slight *click*.

"All the security is really just for show," she told him with a throaty chuckle. "Nothing here's worth a penny, of course, and any one of the employees would blow your head off in an instant if you were to go wandering around. But you wouldn't want to wander around, would you, Mr. Anders?"

He smiled at her. "Of course not."

"The director was right," she said as they walked past a long line of cubicles, none of which bore a nameplate to identify its occupant.

"Right about what?"

"You *are* a dangerous rogue."

"He said that? But I've never met the man."

"No," she agreed, "I don't believe you have. But he was good friends with your mentor, Trace Michelson."

Is this true? Jake asked the Sim.

"Yes," the Sim confirmed. *"I did my postdoctoral work under John Mitchell at Duke University. Agent Lane did some work for him as well, while I was still alive."*

Small world.

"Hardly. John was the best nanotech man around at the time. He taught me a great deal. In more ways than you might expect."

This last comment was left hanging as they reached the end of the corridor and walked through yet another set of glass doors and into a small waiting area. There was no receptionist or secretary here, just a few chairs, a table between them stacked with several dog-eared copies of National Geographic Magazine, and a few leggy plants.

Lottie walked through the waiting area and knocked on the wooden door at one side, then opened it a crack and stuck her head inside. "Mr. Anders for you, Director," she announced with a smile, then turned back to Jake and said, "It was a pleasure to meet you, Mr. Anders. I hope we'll be seeing more of you in the future." And with that, she turned on her four-inch stiletto heels and disappeared into cubicle-land.

"Please, Mr. Anders," came a voice from within the office, "come in." There was a muffled cough and the sound of shuffling papers as Jake opened the door.

The office was far smaller than Jake had expected—much smaller than Haddon's office at the Trust. It was, however, warmly decorated in silks of red and gold, with black-lacquered furniture and a few simple wall hangings. But it was neither the silks nor the furniture that caught his attention. Sitting on the edge of the carved Japanese desk was a delicate bonsai cherry tree. Jake couldn't help but look twice.

"Recognize it?" asked the white-haired man who stood behind the desk.

"I…." Jake was momentarily at a loss for words. "Yes. I think I do."

"It's the same tree, I can assure you. I had always admired it," John Mitchell explained, looking up at Jake and offering him a warm smile. "I bought it for him years ago. Taught him how to prune and tend to it. As always, he did a better job than I ever could." His expression became wistful. "It arrived here after his death. No note. Nothing. I figured it was Trina who sent it, but she never mentioned it. Nor did I, for that matter. It was a difficult time for all of us."

John Mitchell was nothing like Jake had expected him to be. Where Haddon was cool and in control, Mitchell appeared affable and relaxed. The contrast was surprising.

"But I'm being rude," Mitchell apologized, offering his hand. "It's good to finally meet you, Jake Anders. I'm John Mitchell, director of the Avadhuta Group." He smiled and shook Jake's hand. "Please," he added, gesturing to a chair in front of the desk, "have a seat."

Mitchell sat down again and gently cleared his throat. His skin was pale, almost translucent. His eyebrows were dark, in stark contrast to his shoulder-length white hair, and Jake wondered if the man had been ill.

"He has been ill for as long as I've known him," the Sim explained. *"Still, he has changed little over the years. I'm pleased to see it."*

"Thank you, sir," Jake replied, sitting down. He should have felt uncomfortable, naked without his weapons. And yet the older man put him at ease, and he relaxed into the chair, leaning back and crossing his legs.

Mitchell glanced at the bonsai tree once more, then back at Jake. "Trace spoke highly of you, you know." He settled into his chair, the edges of his mouth still set in a smile. "He hoped that we would meet someday. He spoke of bringing you here, to work in the lab, once the Resurrection chip had been perfected. He thought we might be able to show you a thing or two about nanobots, his newest obsession at the time."

"Nanobots?" Jake inquired. "I didn't realize that Trace was interested in them."

"He was fascinated by them." Mitchell's eyes lit with excitement, and Jake could hear the passion in his voice.

"I've followed some of the research," Jake offered. "Johns Hopkins started trials a few months ago on some artery-scraping devices. Looks promising."

"Indeed. Trace Michelson was one of the first scientists to suggest that we could use tiny machines to float around in the body and 'clean up the mess', so to speak. But I digress." Mitchell appeared contrite. "You didn't come here to talk shop, did you?"

Jake hadn't wanted to change topics—he was interested in learning more about Trace's work—but he didn't want to press the issue. Not yet, at least. "I'm not sure why I came here, to be honest with you," he replied.

"I'm sure that you're more than a bit curious about why I sent Agent Klein to track you down in Nepal."

"You could say that."

"You know the basics," Mitchell continued as he studied Jake's face with apparent interest. "The Avadhuta Group and the Trust were once sister organizations. Government sponsored, although they operated with little government oversight."

"That's what Klein told me." Jake's tone was cautious, and he shifted in his seat, crossing his arms over his chest.

"I certainly understand your misgivings about hearing this information," Mitchell said. "It must have been quite a surprise for you to hear that the organization you've been a member of for nearly ten years is not what you believed it to be."

"I'm not sure that I believe Klein's version of the facts." Jake schooled his expression. He was already far too comfortable with Mitchell, too vulnerable, he knew. "How do I know this isn't some test of my loyalties? Or maybe that *your* organization is the rogue here, not the Trust."

"Those are reasonable concerns, and I'd be surprised if you didn't voice them. I'm happy to answer any questions you may have, if that will assist you in your assessment of the situation," Mitchell offered. "I'll do my best to be forthcoming with you, although you'll understand that I cannot divulge any information that might place my people at risk."

"I understand."

There was a knock on the door. Mitchell's assistant placed a tea set on the desk.

"Thank you," said Mitchell.

"You're welcome, sir," the young man said. "Please let me know if there is anything else I can get for you."

Mitchell poured two glasses of tea, then offered one to Jake, who took the tea, thanked the other man, and inhaled the steam. King of Green Masa: Trace's favorite.

"I am surprised that you recognized it," said the Sim.

Jake, once again reminded of the dream from the night before, did not immediately reply. Instead, he sipped the delicate tea, savoring the headiness of the aroma.

"Delicious," he acknowledged with a nod.

"I'm glad you appreciate it." Mitchell took a sip from his own cup. "Unfortunately, my stash has been depleted over the years. This is just about all that remains of the last gift Trace gave me—my government salary is hardly enough to afford the cost to restock."

Jake gathered his thoughts as he drank. He had plenty of questions for Trace's former mentor, but the man had set him off-kilter. He was either a genuinely gracious person or an excellent actor.

"How did you first meet Trace?" Jake decided that the more questions he asked, the more likely he would be to successfully gauge the man's truthfulness.

Mitchell exhaled and closed his eyes for a brief moment. "I met him when he was a young teenager, nipping at the heels of his grandfather, Alfred. Trace was already an impressive intellect at the tender age of fourteen, mind you. He asked me if he could volunteer in my lab at Carolina during the summers. How could I resist? He later came to attend Duke and continued to work with me as a doctoral candidate."

"What was your relationship with the Trust?"

"Under Alfred Michelson's direction?"

Jake nodded.

"Alfred founded the Trust during the time Trace worked in my lab. It began as a contract facility, doing work that the CIA could not. Later on, most of the funding came from the government. Alfred's interests and the government's were very closely aligned. I myself worked with Alfred as a consultant of sorts—advising him on the construction of the first laboratory buildings, assisting him in training the first 'executives', as Alfred liked to call them."

Jake raised an eyebrow.

"Oh, no." Mitchell chuckled, putting his cup down. "I knew nothing about the cloak and dagger business back then. I just advised him on scientific issues, suggested potential recruits, that sort of thing. I didn't learn this end of the business until I left Duke to come work for the CIA, a few years before Alfred's murder." He spoke the last few words as almost an afterthought.

"Murder?"

"Yes," Mitchell replied. "Murder."

"But we were told—"

"You were told what everyone else was told, of course," Mitchell interrupted. "It was a lie. Alfred Michelson was murdered. His murderer was never found."

Jake frowned.

Did you know of this too?

"Yes," replied the Sim. *"Trace was convinced that his grandfather's death had been planned. He was unfortunately never able to prove it."*

"A few years before Alfred's death," Mitchell continued, "Trace left Duke to set up a lab in Chicago. After Alfred died, Trace took over as director of the Trust. Later, of course, Trace himself was assassinated, and Charles Haddon replaced Trace when Trina refused."

"So the 'split' happened after Trace's death?"

"Yes," replied Mitchell, "although it wasn't a sudden thing, as you might expect. Over time, the Trust just began to operate more and more independently of the CIA, until the remaining ties to the government eroded entirely."

"This was Haddon's doing?"

"It certainly wasn't Trace's intention to lead the Trust in that direction, if that's what you're getting at." Mitchell sounded somewhat offended. "Trace, and his grandfather before him, saw the Trust as a unique opportunity to accomplish real good in the world by preventing the misuse of technology. They only took life when there was no other option. They abhorred violence."

Jake recalled his sparring match with Trace and snorted.

Mitchell offered Jake a knowing smile. "Surely you, Agent Anders, understand that it is not a contradiction to avoid violence and still be trained to defend oneself."

"Yes. Of course." It was something Trace had tried to teach him, but that he'd initially failed to grasp. "But if all of this is true," Jake continued, "why did the government just sit back and watch Haddon commandeer the Trust for his own purposes? Why not just move in and take over the operation?"

"Good question," Mitchell answered, refilling their teacups. "And one I don't know the answer to, at least in as far as why the government didn't immediately step in. Later on, my supervisors were more inclined to see what technology the Trust had developed, to determine if it was something from which they might derive a benefit. At least, when they became aware of Project Resurrection, that is."

"They didn't know about the project until Haddon became director?"

"Apparently not. I myself was unaware of Trace's work with the Sims until after his death," Mitchell explained. "He hinted around about it, but I believe he wanted to show me the finished product. He was quite proud of his work, and quite the perfectionist."

"An exaggeration," Jake heard the Sim say.

Right. Jake stifled a laugh.

"I still find it hard to believe your bosses would have waited nearly five years to interfere."

"It didn't take them long to realize they'd made a mistake," Mitchell admitted. "But by then, Haddon had built up the organization's defenses to the point that they were nearly impenetrable. I'm sure Agent Klein explained that we've tried to infiltrate the Trust over the years."

"He said something about neutralizing agents through some sort of reprogramming."

Mitchell's expression became hard. "We've lost too many good men and women to that process, thanks to Vasalia Synchack."

Jake thought about Cathy and Krista and repressed a shiver.

For a moment Mitchell said nothing. Then, appearing to have made up his mind about something, he said, "Trace trusted you, Agent Anders. He believed you to be not only an excellent agent and scientist but a good man, as well."

Jake ignored the compliment, instead waiting for the other man to continue.

"I know that Trace gave you the Resurrection chip," Mitchell said, as if the information weighed heavily upon him. "I don't expect you to confirm this. But from what I understand of the Sim technology and of Trace himself, your chip is the only one that contains the sum total of Trace's experiences and understanding."

He knows what you are.

"Apparently so," the Sim replied. *"But then, he was always very perceptive."*

"Jacob Anders," Mitchell continued, "I have known you personally only a few minutes, and yet I place my trust in Trace's choice of a host. I, therefore, trust *you*."

"What difference does your trusting me make? Do you believe I'll help you?"

"Yes," Mitchell replied, "although you'd be unwise to accept my word as gospel. That Trace would have taken the time to train you means you are far too intelligent and cunning to take my word for it. You must discover the truth for yourself."

"Then what do you want from me?" Jake was once more keenly aware of how unprotected he was here, of how much he'd risked simply in coming. All Mitchell's talk of trust and being worthy of the Sim made him uncomfortable and suspicious.

He waited for Mitchell to bring up the subject of the Sim chip again, but he did not. Instead, he said, "For now, I want only for you to consider what I've told you and draw your own conclusions." Then he pulled open a drawer on his desk, withdrew a small padded envelope, and handed it to Jake.

Jake took the envelope and looked at it with a frown. "What is this?"

"Something Trace gave to me, years ago, for safekeeping," Mitchell explained. "He gave it to me with the instructions that, were you ever to come to me seeking answers, I was to give it to you."

Jake turned the envelope over, ran his forefinger between its edges, and opened one end. He reached inside and pulled out a small object wrapped in delicate white silk. He was immediately reminded of the silk scarf Trace had often worn over his suit, years ago. He gently unwound the silk to reveal a pocket-sized silver dagger with six small jewels embedded in its hilt.

For a moment Jake said nothing, but just stared at the incredible workmanship of the weapon. It was very old and probably very valuable. He ran his fingers with reverence over the flat side of the blade.

"It's beautiful," he said, not caring if Mitchell saw the emotional impact the knife had on him.

"He told me to tell you something, as well." Jake looked up into Mitchell's face and thought he saw true sadness there.

"He told me to tell you that the truth is within your soul, Jake, and that you need look no further for answers."

Jake took a deep breath. "How do I contact you?" he asked.

"*I* will contact *you*."

"Through Klein?"

"No," Mitchell answered, "not this time."

Jake raised an eyebrow.

"I still have one agent working within the walls of the Trust who has not been compromised. That agent has risked a great deal to remain in such a dangerous situation. That agent will contact you when the time is right."

chapter thirteen

On the Brink

We do not learn by experience but by our capacity for experience.

—Buddha

JAKE arrived back in Chicago in much the same way he'd left, by driving straight through the night. When he made it back to his apartment in the early morning, he was far too keyed up to sleep, and the gift that Trace had left with Mitchell tugged at something deep inside him—something far deeper than he was willing to admit.

"That dagger has been in the Michelson Family for generations," explained the Sim as Jake withdrew the package from his jacket pocket.

Why would he give it to me, then?

"Jake, you know the answer."

My penchant for knife throwing, perhaps?

The Sim remained silent.

Jake placed the silver dagger on the kitchen table, still wrapped in its silk. But as he moved away from the table, the edge of the silk caught on his watchband, and the dagger flipped out of its cocoon. He reached out to stop the dagger from falling onto the floor, but caught the weapon by the razor-sharp edge of its blade and sliced open his index finger in the effort.

"Damn!"

He put the knife down and strode over to the kitchen sink to wash the cut and assess the damage. The gash was deep, running the better part of an inch along his finger and having cut close to the bone.

He pressed the edges of the wound together, recalling his otherworldly conversation in Nepal about healing techniques as he watched it bleed. The attack in Union Station and what Dr. Carroll had told him later about his femoral artery healing itself left him considering the possibility that Trace, and the monks, might be onto something.

Blood seeped from the gash into the white porcelain sink and mixed with the water in a swirl of red. Figuring that he had nothing to lose, he focused his attention on the wound and imagined it closing as one might close a zipper. "Heal," he added for effect, remembering Trace's belief that an audible mantra helped maintain focus during meditation.

He didn't expect much and, for a split second, inwardly kicked himself for being stupid enough to believe that a thing like self-directed healing was possible. Kicked himself, that was, until he saw the cut seal itself, leaving the skin unblemished.

What the hell...?

For a moment he just stood there, staring at his finger in amazement. Then, his curiosity getting the better of him, he picked up the dagger and cut into the palm of his hand. Not too deep. Just enough to make it bleed.

The initial sensation of the cold blade against his skin was followed in short order by a sharp burning sensation. He narrowed his eyes and muttered, "Heal," once more. The wound did just that. In less than thirty seconds, his palm was unmarred and completely healed. The only evidence of the injury remaining was the blood that had dripped onto the floor by the sink.

Shit.

This revelation was followed by near-frenzied cutting over various places on his body. By the time he'd finished his little "experiment," he found that he had the ability to heal even the deeper slashes in seconds, without the verbal command. Each time he cut himself, the pain was less intense than before, although the wounds he inflicted were progressively deeper.

Unbelievable!

He leaned back against the kitchen wall and considered the dagger once more. The six jewels glittered in the bright light; the blade was covered with blood—his own blood.

He turned the knife around and plunged it into an area on his arm that he knew wouldn't threaten any major arteries. Then he jabbed the knife into his thigh. Both of these wounds, although deeper, healed neatly and without leaving a mark. Emboldened by his success, he had raised the dagger, holding its hilt with both hands and pointing it toward his chest when he heard, "What the hell?"

Greyson, who had let himself inside the unlocked apartment, ran over and grabbed Jake's arm just in time to prevent him from driving the dagger into his chest. This move, however, only succeeded in pushing the dagger into Jake's abdomen. Jake looked down at his blood-soaked clothes and then up at Grey.

"Jake!" Grey shouted, his face white with shock as he pressed his hand over the wound on Jake's gut. "Are you fucking trying to kill yourself?"

Jake could see fear in Grey's eyes, and he smiled reassuringly while he tried to decide how he'd explain the drops of blood on the floor and the red smears on the table and sink. "Got cut up a bit," he told Grey with a laugh. In retrospect, he realized he sounded borderline hysterical, but at that moment he couldn't help himself. The initial pain was followed by a sense of near-euphoria, and he was almost giddy at the implications of his discovery.

"I need to call this in—we need to get you to Dr. Carroll or to a hospital. *Now.*"

"No."

"What do you mean, 'no'? Do you *want* to die?" Grey looked horrified.

"Move your hand."

"No way—you'll bleed out. If you think I'm going to let you—"

Jake pushed Grey off of him. The two scuffled a bit before Grey realized that Jake was no longer bleeding.

Jake lifted his shirt. There was no wound where the knife had entered moments before.

"What the...?" Grey began. His brow knitted and he shook his head, as if he didn't believe what he was seeing.

Jake bent down to retrieve the knife from the floor.

"What the *fuck* are you doing, Jake?" Grey demanded.

Jake reached for the dagger, but Grey moved to block him, knocking the hilt around in the process. Jake grabbed the knife by the blade and ended up with another cut to show for it.

"Stop!" yelled Grey, trying to drag Jake to the sink to tend to the new cut. Jake held his ground, and when Grey finally managed to turn Jake's hand over, no trace of the wound remained.

"What the hell, Jake. Where's the cut?" He grabbed both of Jake's bloodied hands, but the skin there was unmarred.

"I can heal my wounds. Without meditation. Watch."

Before Grey could stop him, Jake jabbed the dagger into his other hand, then withdrew the blade. Blood oozed with the initial stab, but the flow ended as the wound sealed itself.

"The internal damage is healed too. It's like a pinprick, then it's gone. Muscle, fascia, skin, nerves, all healed in seconds. Deeper cuts can take a minute or so, but it's the same."

Grey was dumbfounded. "How long have you been able to do this?"

"Since this morning."

Grey stared at his friend.

"Grey, do you know what this means?" Jake was almost unable to contain his excitement.

Grey raised an eyebrow as if afraid to hear the answer. "No" was all he said.

"It means that Trace could have survived the gunshot wound."

This was met by renewed silence and a deep scowl. Finally, Grey said, "Jake, stabbing yourself and healing those wounds is very different than repairing a major organ. You can't survive a gunshot to the heart."

"Why not? If Trace had the same ability, only a bullet to the brain would've killed him—and only because he wouldn't have been able to think clearly enough to direct the healing process. But Trace was shot in the *heart*, Grey, not the brain. He could have survived the wound."

Grey's expression turned hard, and there was something else in his eyes—something Jake could not quite read. Pain, perhaps. "No, he couldn't," he said. "He didn't *want* to survive being shot."

"What?"

"You heard me. He wanted to die, Jake."

Jake grabbed Grey by the front of his shirt and pushed him back hard against the kitchen counter. "What the hell do you mean? And how would *you* know what Trace wanted?"

"Jake, you're obsessed. You're delusional. Trace is dead. Get that through your fucking hard head!"

"Don't you see?" Jake continued, his voice rising to match Grey's. "He could've survived the gunshot wound. He was *much* better at healing techniques than I am. If I can do *this*, think of what *he* could have accomplished!"

"Jake, he wanted to die!"

"What? How the fuck do you know that?"

"I know because he asked me to kill him."

For a moment, Jake just stared at Grey, unable to speak. Then, his voice returning, he stammered, "H-he… what?"

"He asked me to kill him." Grey's face was like granite, his eyes tortured. "Hell, he *ordered* me to do it."

"What are you saying?" Jake demanded with growing dismay.

"Dammit, Jake," Grey snapped, "*I* was the one who shot Trace. *I killed him!*"

chapter fourteen

Reality Bites

Zen is like looking for spectacles that are sitting on your nose.

—Zen saying

JAKE just stared at Grey, uncomprehending. Then he said in a low, controlled voice, "I don't believe you."

"No? You think I'd *lie* about something like this?"

"You couldn't have killed him. He was one of *us*."

"Yeah," Grey replied. "He was one of us. Hell, I admired the guy. You think I *wanted* to kill him?"

"I don't believe you," Jake repeated in a hollow voice.

"Do you remember that day, Jake?"

"How could I forget it?" Jake replied solemnly. "I met you at the entrance to the Michelsons' estate. We heard screams and we ran. He was in Trina's arms, bleeding. I tried to save him…."

"Didn't you ever wonder why I didn't ride with you that day?" Grey's jaw was tight.

"I don't know. I guess I just figured you were picking Trina up from her apartment."

"She spent the night out there, remember?"

Jake didn't answer.

"I didn't pick her up because Trace set it up so that she'd be out there already," Grey continued, a muscle in his cheek twitching "He wanted me to be alone. He didn't want anyone to know. He set the whole thing up."

Jake threw Grey against the wall and punched him hard on the chin. "Shut up!"

Grey didn't move. "Trace's murderer was never found," he continued, "because *he* arranged it all. He knew you couldn't do it. He asked me to do it because—"

"Shut up!" Jake shouted again. He grabbed Grey by the collar and pushed him harder against the wall.

"He told me exactly where to shoot him and the type of bullet to use. He told me to shoot him through the heart. He didn't want to survive, *he wanted to die*."

"No," Jake growled, although he eased the pressure on Grey's neck as he spoke.

"It's the God's honest truth. Why the hell would I lie about something like this?"

Silence, and then: "How *could* you?"

"How could I what? Kill my friend? The only brother of the woman I love? My teacher?" Grey hissed. "I did it because Trace *ordered* me to do it. I didn't want to do it, believe me, I didn't." He paused for a moment, swallowing hard. "It was torture to watch him die in Trina's arms, to die in front of me, knowing that I was the one who pulled the trigger. So don't go telling me he's alive, Jake, because he's not. Nothing could bring him back from that—he made *damn* sure of it. *I* made damn sure of it."

Jake let go of Grey. *Is it true?* he asked the Sim, not sure if he really wanted to hear the answer. His heart pounded in his ears; he felt sick.

"Yes," the Sim replied. *"Trace ordered Grey to shoot him."*

How could you even know? You were created before he was shot. This whole thing is—

"I know Trace's thoughts," the Sim interrupted. *"He planned it months before it happened."*

I refuse to believe he's dead.

"That's your prerogative, of course."

"Does Trina know?" Jake asked, mastering his emotions once more.

"What? Do you think I'm fucking crazy? No, she doesn't, and you're not going to tell her, either."

Jake just stared at Grey. He had no idea what to say. The entire concept—that Trace had planned his death and ordered one of his own to shoot him—was more than Jake could fathom. He walked over to the couch and sat down heavily, his shoulders slumping, his chin on his chest.

"He was only carrying out the mission, Jake," the Sim said.

I know, I know. But why?

"That, I don't know."

And why the fuck didn't you tell me?

The Sim did not respond.

He let out a long, slow breath and looked up at Grey, who was still standing and watching him. Waiting.

"No," Jake said, at last. "I'm not going to tell Trina."

Grey exhaled audibly, then sat down across from Jake. "I'm sorry," he said in an undertone. "I'm sorry to be the one to tell you. I'm sorry I…." His voice trailed off and he just shook his head.

"You only did what he asked you to do." His voice was flat, unemotional.

"You loved him, didn't you?" Grey asked. "You still love him."

Jake said nothing.

Grey shifted uncomfortably in his seat and looked down at his bloodstained hands. "You can't tell anyone about this, Jake."

"About the healing?"

Grey nodded.

"Why not?"

Grey pulled a few sheets of paper from his back pocket. "We need to talk. It's important."

"Sure," Jake said. "What's up?"

"Go shower and change. I'll wait," he said, ignoring the question.

"But—"

"I'll clean up a bit," Grey interrupted. "Take a shower. I'll make us some coffee."

"Okay," Jake agreed, although he didn't really want to.

"It's fine," Grey reassured him. "Go ahead. I'll be here when you finish up."

JAKE walked back into the living room about twenty minutes later. With the shower and a clean change of clothes, there was no evidence of any of the self-inflicted wounds.

"Shit," Grey said as he looked over his friend with growing wonder, "you really are a piece of work."

Jake laughed. "So give me the bad news."

"How do you know it's bad?" Grey countered.

"I know that look, Lane."

"This is the decrypted information from the Thebes file," Grey said as he handed Jake the papers. "They're Trace's notes from the Project Resurrection clinical trials."

"How did you get this?"

"Trina."

"Trina?" asked Jake.

"Apparently she's been taking lessons from the executives. Hacked into Synchack's files."

"Sweet. And she got her hands on this before you did too."

"Or you," Grey reminded Jake.

They sat down on the balcony, and Jake poured them both hot coffee as he read through the notes. It was Jake who spoke first. "So if I don't remove my Sim chip, I'll go insane?"

"Seems that way."

"I'll have to think about it."

"What? Think about going insane? You really *are* too delusional to know what's good for you."

"There's no guarantee one way or the other," Jake snapped. "It's my choice."

"There's something else bothering you."

"You mean other than finding out my best friend killed the one man I…." Jake couldn't finish the sentence.

"So you admit it, then?" Grey's voice was kind.

"That I was in love with the guy?" He looked back at Grey and set his cup on the table. "Yeah. I guess I was."

Grey chuckled. "I think you were both obsessed with each other, you know."

"Whatever."

"He's dead, Jake." Grey sighed. "I'm sorry."

"There *is* one way to test my theory…."

Grey scowled. "No way in *hell*," he warned.

"Come on, Grey, you did it once, you can do it again."

"No way am I going to shoot you through the heart to prove your theory."

"You just might have to, given this shit." Jake tossed the papers onto the middle of the table and stared at them with a glum expression.

"Go find someone else to do it. I don't want any part of this insanity."

"I'm sure Pilkington would do it." Jake laughed and leaned back in his chair.

"Fucker's the worst shot. He'll hit you in the head."

"Well, if my so-called friend won't do it, I guess I'll have to settle."

"Fuck off," Grey responded, beginning to relax once more.

Jake looked out over the city. He wasn't sure what to make of Trace's notes, especially not after his conversation with Mitchell. Would someone who'd abhorred violence have carried out such dangerous experiments and euthanized test subjects?

Maybe Mitchell didn't know Trace as well as he thought. Or maybe I am going crazy. Jake wished he could tell Grey about his meeting with Mitchell, hash it out with him.

"Jake, what are you keeping from me? You know you can trust me."

"If I *was* keeping something from you, why the hell would I tell you? The way things went down in Switzerland, I'm not sure I should trust you, anyhow."

"You trusted me enough a minute ago to ask me to shoot you," Grey pointed out.

"Which you won't."

Grey let the comment slide. Then, casually refilling his coffee cup, he said simply, "You *can* trust me. I'm like you."

"Like me?" Jake asked, with a bitter laugh. "And how's that?"

"Ares," Grey answered with a tap of a finger to his earlobe.

"Yeah, and what about your Sim?"

"What you told me about. You know, talking to your Sim, stuff like that." Grey hesitated, then continued, "I'm getting it too."

"You're getting it… you mean, the Ares Sim is talking to *you*, like the Trace Sim talks to me?"

Grey nodded. "Yeah. It was creepy at first."

Jake remained silent, allowing Grey to finish.

"Haven't told anyone, especially that psycho Synchack. I mean, the way Haddon's been looking at *you*—"

"Haddon sent you here today, didn't he?" Jake interrupted.

Grey pursed his lips. "Yeah," he admitted. "He wants me to keep an eye on you."

"Why you?" Jake asked. "I mean, if he's interested in me because of my Sim, why would he treat you any differently than he treats me? You're just another test subject."

Grey stared at his cup for a moment, then released his breath from between his lips like someone blowing out a candle. "He treats me differently," Grey explained, "because he thinks his reprogramming technique worked on me."

Jake raised his head in surprise. "What the fuck? He tried to *neutralize* you? When?"

"When he thought I might be working for the other side. It was right around the time of the mission in Union Station."

"What?"

"That mission I went on for several weeks—I was being reprogrammed."

"Did it work?"

"No."

"Why not?"

"The Sim chip prevents the drugs and the other techniques from working—neutralizes the effects. I just had to pretend to be a lap dog."

"How would you even *know* it didn't take? I mean, that's the whole point, right? You're not supposed to know...." Jake felt cold inside.

This is bad. Really bad. Really fucking bad.

"I know it didn't take because I'm not insane," Grey explained. Jake raised a skeptical eyebrow. "I also know because Ares told me," Grey added. "He talked me through it while it was happening. He fed me the answers Synchack was looking for to make sure the programming worked."

"So Haddon has no clue the chip saved your ass?"

"I think he tried the technique on me in part because he wanted to find out if it would," Grey replied. "I was his guinea pig."

Is his story true?

"It's quite likely," the Trace Sim said. *"From my understanding of Synchack's technique, it wouldn't work on you either. Trace anticipated just this type of interference."*

Silence settled between the two men as Jake sipped his now ice-cold coffee. He heard Mitchell's voice echo through his mind.

"I still have one agent working within the walls of the Trust who has not been compromised. That agent has risked a great deal to remain in such a dangerous situation. That agent will contact you when the time is right."

"Shit, Grey!" Jake exclaimed, spitting a mouthful of coffee back into the cup. "You're my contact."

"Didn't take long for you to figure that out, did it?" Grey replied, his voice heavy with sarcasm. Then, clenching his jaw, he added, "Yeah. I'm your contact. I've been working with Mitchell since a few days after Trace's death."

chapter fifteen

Descent into Madness

One may defeat a thousand obstacles and adversaries, yet he who defeats the enemies within is the noblest victor.

—Shakyamuni

GREYSON LANE peered into the director's office. "Sir, you wanted to see me?"

Haddon looked up, closed the report that he'd been reading, and gave Grey a placid smile. "Yes, Agent Lane, please have a seat," he said, "and shut the door behind you, if you don't mind."

"Of course, sir," Grey replied, closing the door and taking a seat in front of the meticulously clean desk. Sunlight streamed into the office through the wooden blinds on the window, and a steaming pot of tea sat between them, ignored.

"What do you have to report?" asked Haddon. The tea set caught his eye, and he took one of the cups and filled it. He did not offer any to his guest.

"I've been tailing Agent Anders as you asked, sir," Grey responded.

"And?"

"And he's been behaving very strangely."

"How so?" Haddon rubbed his beard, then picked up the cup. The tea had steeped too long, and he frowned at the bitter taste. He replaced the cup and leaned back, lips pursed together in eager anticipation.

"I tailed him last night," Grey explained. "He drove his car around for hours, running errands."

"And what's so unusual about that?"

"After he went shopping for food, he drove to an all-night pharmacy and bought some bandages."

"Bandages?"

"Yes. Apparently he couldn't find the right kind at the grocery store, or maybe it's that he just couldn't find enough there. He ended up buying piles of them—different shapes, sizes, some gauze, tape—it was almost as if he were preparing for a major trauma."

"Anything else?"

"I went to visit him this morning to give him a ride to work, and when I got there, he was covered in blood," Grey explained. "It was everywhere. On the floor, the table, in the sink...." His voice trailed off, his face registering deep concern.

"Go on," Haddon said, leaning in toward Grey.

"Agent Anders was cutting himself, sir."

"Cutting himself?"

"Yes, sir," Grey responded. "He had taken a knife and was cutting his arms and legs." He paused for a moment, then continued, "Sir, I'm worried about him."

"Do you believe he is a danger to himself or to others?"

"I'm not sure," Grey admitted. "None of the cuts were life-threatening. But as far as harming anyone else, I just don't know."

"Did he give a reason for behaving in such a manner?"

"That was strange too," Grey replied with a tight expression. "He told me he needed to 'feel' something. I asked him what he meant by that, but he wouldn't tell me. He started to get agitated when I pressed him on it, so I dropped it."

"I see," Haddon said. "Thank you, Greyson. You've done well. Keep an eye on him and report back to me if anything new develops."

Grey got up. "I'll have the full report on your desk in an hour, sir."

"No need, Agent Lane. Let's keep this between you and me—for now, at least."

"Of course, sir," Grey replied, nodding and walking out of the office.

Haddon looked back down at the file on his desk, opened it up once again, and put two fingers to his lips as he contemplated its contents.

THE next day Jake and Grey worked in the DNA lab, continuing the experiment from the week before. Grey looked over at Jake and frowned.

"What?" Jake scowled and went back to his work.

"Nothing," Grey replied. "Just worried about you, that's all."

"Fuck off," Jake told him in a low voice. "I don't need anyone worryin' about me."

Grey looked back at his computer screen.

A voice came over the loudspeaker. "Agent Anders, please report to Dr. Carroll for drug screening."

Jake glanced over at Grey and shrugged; all of the Trust's agents submitted to random drug testing periodically.

Grey still said nothing.

Jake exhaled, making no attempt to hide his irritation, tossing his lab coat onto a chair. He headed for the Trust's medical facility without so much as a word to Grey.

"AGENT Anders, it's good to see you," Dr. Carroll said as Jake walked through the etched double doors of the clinic a few minutes later. "Please come in and have a seat."

Carroll smiled at Jake, noting with some interest the long sleeves he wore despite the weather outside, which was positively scorching. "Agent Anders," she said, "I'll need you to roll up your sleeve for me so I can take a blood sample." He complied, rolling his right shirtsleeve above the elbow to reveal a heavily bandaged arm. The gauze was spotted with blood, which had seeped through the wrappings.

"You've injured yourself." She hoped her expression didn't betray her shock at the sight of the damage to Anders's arm. "Perhaps the other arm would be a better choice."

He rolled up the other sleeve, and it was much the same—bandaged and bloody.

"Agent Anders," she asked him with growing distress, "what happened to your arms?"

"I guess I got a bit carried away with an experiment I was conducting." He looked sheepish.

She smiled kindly at him, doing her utmost to remain professional in spite of her alarm, then took his arm and began to unwrap the bandages. Slash marks covered his forearm like angry red tattoos. She had no doubt the wounds were self-inflicted.

"These cuts are infected. Please let me clean these for you and re-dress them."

Jake shrugged noncommittally, then watched in silence as she began to clean and rewrap his arms. "I'm concerned about you, Jake," she told him, hoping she would reassure him. "You know that you can always speak to me in confidence if you're having any difficulties you feel you cannot resolve on your own."

"Thanks. I may take you up on that," Jake replied, his tone casual.

She watched him shift awkwardly in the chair. She had never seen him so distressed, so… rattled.

After finishing her work, she picked up a syringe from a nearby table. "I'm going to give you a tetanus shot," she explained. "I'm also going to give you another booster—it's similar to the one I gave you before you first received the Sim chip."

"Sure."

"I'd also like to run some tests, if you don't mind—other than the drug screen. Is that all right with you?"

"Sure," he repeated.

She pulled up a cart with a sample cup, scissors, needles, and a few vials of liquid with labels sporting only numbers on them. While she drew his blood, she continued to ask him questions. "Are you still conversing with your Sim, other than in the simulation chamber?"

"Yes," Jake admitted, "although Trace doesn't pop up in front of me anymore while I'm awake, if that's what you mean."

"Really?"

"Yeah, but he does show up in my dreams at night. It's a little weird," he added.

"How so?" She prepared one of the syringes, then prepped his arm and injected him.

"I can smell his aftershave, feel his touch. It's like he's *there*, in the room with me. Much more vivid than my usual dreams. Almost like I could reach out and touch him."

"That's normal," she lied, doing her best to reassure him. "The Sim is a part of your consciousness, after all."

He appeared relieved.

"Jake," she asked, "the cuts on your arms… are you cutting yourself to make sure you're awake and not dreaming?"

He appeared to hesitate, then said, "Yeah, I guess you could say that. I don't really mean to, but I can't seem to help myself." He rubbed his eyes with one hand. "I know it sounds crazy…."

"It's normal to be concerned about your mental health." She labeled a blood sample, then picked up a light and shined it in his eyes briefly. "But I can think of better ways of coping with the stress of sharing your mind with the Sim than cutting yourself."

"The cuts heal when I tell them to." He sounded defensive.

"They heal?" She blinked, her professional veneer failing her for just an instant.

"See?" He pointed to his arm next to the large welt she had just bandaged.

She smiled back at him with eyes full of patient understanding, but she couldn't help but think of Trace's notes, knowing that altered realities were a possibility with the Sim chip.

"Jake," she told him as she injected him with the last hypodermic, "the boosters should help you distinguish reality from dreams—they're meant to work in concert with the Sim. If they don't work, however, I'm going to need to remove the chip and readminister the inoculations."

He stood up abruptly, clearly disturbed at the prospect of losing the chip. His eyes darted to the door as if he were looking for a way to escape.

She put her hand on his shoulder to reassure him. "I would only remove the chip for a week or so—just long enough to give the inoculations time to work," she explained. "I'll personally remove and store the chip. No one else need know I've removed it."

He paused, then nodded and said, "Okay. But only as a last resort, and only for a week."

"Of course," she comforted him, looking him directly in the eyes. She knew she couldn't guarantee anything, but she needed him to stay calm. "But Jake," she reminded him, "you'll need to be honest with me. Please. I'm here to help."

"Thanks. I appreciate that," he answered.

AN HOUR later, Stephanie Carroll sat in front of Charles Haddon's desk, holding her tablet. She tapped the screen several times and frowned.

"What were your findings regarding Agent Anders?" Haddon asked, his face inscrutable.

"He is, as you suspected, cutting himself. He presented with deep cuts on his arms, his legs, and his torso. Nothing life-threatening. I treated him for minor infections and dressed the wounds. I also drew blood samples and gave him some of the booster shots prescribed in Trace Michelson's protocol for Project Resurrection."

"Then he does have some of the symptoms described in the document I sent to you?" Haddon appeared pleased with the news.

"He may," she replied. "But the cutting behavior could be a sign of mental illness rather than a sign of the psychotropic issues that were outlined in Trace's notes. I'll continue to administer the boosters without removing the Sim and see if his symptoms abate."

"And if they do not?"

"Then the chip will have to be removed permanently," she replied.

"And what is the likelihood that the symptoms will completely disappear when the chip is removed?"

"According to Trace Michelson's notes, he will most likely return to normal, with no permanent side effects."

"Excellent," Haddon responded without hesitation. "I'd hate to lose such a valuable executive. There are few agents with the combat skills, intelligence, and scientific expertise of Mr. Anders."

"Certainly," she agreed.

"And what if Michelson's assumptions were wrong—what is the likelihood that the chip could be implanted in another agent?"

She had already considered the possibility, and she shook her head as she spoke. "From Dr. Michelson's notes, it appears highly unlikely that the chip could be reprogrammed for another host. The Sim was configured specifically for Agent Anders's brain structure and electrical patterns."

Haddon appeared to consider this information for a moment but did not pursue the issue further. "Dr. Synchack has decrypted some additional information that may be of assistance to you in your treatment of Agent Anders. You should have access to that data now. It appears that Michelson had some success with 'problem' hosts by rebooting their Sims."

She knew he was watching her to see how she responded to the suggestion. She glanced down at her tablet, tapped it, and read the latest information, happy not to have to look him in the eyes. What she saw on the screen, however, was far more troubling than facing Haddon. She looked back up again, knowing her expression betrayed her shock. "But that process appears to require the host be rendered clinically dead to be effective," she countered. "The risk—"

"I am aware of the risk, Doctor," he interrupted. "However, in his current state, Anders is of little value to this organization, and worse, he's a potential danger to himself. I will not risk damaging the chip." There was a steely determination in his voice as his dark eyes met hers.

"So how about it?" he pressed when she didn't reply. "Can we reboot Agent Anders's Sim, Doctor?"

"We may be able to accomplish it in a controlled environment," she said, although it pained her to admit it. It was risky—far too risky for her taste. "The heart, as well as the brain itself, would need to 'die'—temporarily, of course. These notes make no mention of how long he needs to be clinically dead before resuscitation." She pursed her lips. "But, Director—"

"But can it be done?"

"Yes, although it would pose a serious risk to Agent Anders." Haddon looked irritated now, and she swallowed hard, knowing she was overstepping her authority.

"You've already explained the risk, Stephanie. Can you determine how long he would need to be kept in stasis before the reboot would be effective?"

"I can probably make those calculations based upon the information in the research notes," she answered.

"And what is his current condition?"

"He's sedated and resting in the medical wing. He'll be released this evening if there are no ill effects from the first round of injections he received today."

"Very good. Continue with the booster protocol for the time being. You have two weeks. If there is no change, we will attempt the reboot process," he told her. "Thank you for your assistance, Dr.

Carroll. Please close the door behind you as you are leaving." She stood up and nodded, then walked out of the room.

ALONE in his office a few moments later, Haddon asked, "Did you hear all that, Vasalia?"

The scientist grunted over the phone line.

"You don't agree?"

"No. I see no reason to wait," Synchack replied. "She is not being forthcoming with you. She did not mention that she must remove Anders's Sim chip for the boosters to achieve the maximum effect."

"So you believe she has already removed it?"

"Not yet. She coddles the fool, waiting for him to make the decision to remove it. But if the chip remains implanted in two weeks and the symptoms have not abated, I will reboot him myself. If he dies, the chip can be implanted in another subject."

"And her concern regarding reimplantation of the Sim?"

Synchack let out a hissing sound. "She is far too conservative, and we have plenty of willing subjects available to test the chip before we attempt the procedure on you."

"Anything more about the location of the backup chip?"

"We're working on retrieving it. If the reboot is successful, we will have it ready for you. If not, we will use Anders's in its place."

"Have you discovered who received the data transmission from the Swiss wafers?"

"Yes," Synchack answered. "And what I have learned is quite interesting. The wafer is transmitting the information to Anders's Sim and to another receiver, most likely the backup chip."

"Understood. Do what you must, Vasalia."

"Krista will be up shortly with the next round of your preimplantation inoculations. You'll receive one more set after this."

JAKE lay in one of the private medical rooms, staring up at the ceiling tiles. In spite of the sedative, his mind was clear. He wondered if this was due to the effects of the Sim that Grey had described.

"Jake, you're playing a dangerous game."

It's my game to play, Jake retorted. *I have people to protect, just like you do.*

"Just like I did."

I have to keep the heat off Grey and Trina. Hell, I have to keep the heat off of all of the agents you hired.

"Why do you believe they're at risk?"

C'mon, Trace. Don't play coy with me—why the hell did you have Grey shoot you? You were obviously protecting someone.

Silence.

You know why Grey shot Trace, don't you?

"I do."

But you're not going to tell me, are you?

The Sim hesitated uncharacteristically. *"Haddon wanted my research to create a new kind of 'executive'—compliant and programmable. I refused."*

Doesn't sound like anything you couldn't have handled.

"I could have handled Haddon," the Sim replied. *"It wasn't, however, only my life that was at risk."*

Trina.

"Precisely," the Sim answered in a low voice.

Bastard threatened to hurt her if you didn't help him, didn't he?

"Yes."

But you could have just disappeared.

"True. But I couldn't force her to do the same."

You could have asked me to help you, you know. I would have.

"I had already placed too many people I cared about in harm's way. This was something I had to do on my own."

So now you understand why this has to be my *way. Are you going to help me, or do I go it alone?*

"Jake, you've used me as your crutch for far too long."

What's that supposed to mean?

"Only that the Sim chip is an illusion. The real technology—my essence, as it were—will still remain with you even if the chip is removed."

Then this was just one elaborate setup, wasn't it? Jake shook his head and let out a breath in an audible hiss. *You're fucking unbelievable, you know.*

Silence.

What's really on the duplicate chip, then?

"Evidence of Haddon's treachery."

Where is it?

"The Michelson family crypt. You'll need the dagger and the three wafers to gain access."

Really not making this easy, are you?

"You would hardly want to see my life's work fall into Haddon's hands, would you? Besides, retrieving it will assist both you and Grey in your plans."

Hell, I'm always up for a challenge. Let's get this show on the road.

THE medical facility's lights had been dimmed, and Jake pretended to sleep. The night nurse came to check on him—probably to see that he was still sedated and sleeping soundly—and he waited until she turned her back to him before slipping out of the bed and knocking her unconscious. After laying her down on one of the empty beds, he removed his bandages and tossed them onto the floor. His arms were unblemished; all of the cuts had disappeared. He left the room, grabbed his clothes from a small closet outside, and buttoned his shirt along the way.

Arriving at the research building a few minutes later, he punched in the code to gain access to the area that housed the Trust's mainframe computer. There, the wafers he and Grey had stolen from the facility in Bern were being housed while the Trust's technicians worked to decrypt the files obtained from the Research Triangle Park facility. He slipped into the room and was about to move toward the computer when one of the tech staff attempted to intercept him. The man was unconscious a moment later.

Jake depressed a latch on the access panel of a custom storage unit, and the panel slid open to reveal a compartment with three wafers resting on a special tray. Pulling on the glove he'd found on the counter, he reached in, and placed the wafers in the padded holder he'd stashed in his pocket. He left without closing the compartment.

The alarm sounded as he got into his car. He tore out of the parking lot and dashed home to get the rest of the equipment he needed to complete the task at hand.

AS JAKE pulled away from the building, a figure in another car watched as a voice came over the tiny receiver in his ear.

"Follow him, Grant."

Grant Schaeffer glanced over at his partner, Theo Pilkington, and grinned. They'd been waiting a long time for this.

"Should I eliminate him, sir?"

"No. Just follow him for now. Report back to me as soon as you ascertain his destination."

"Yes, Director Haddon." He had no intention of following Haddon's orders. It was payback time.

BACK at his apartment, Jake stripped off his clothes and slipped into a lightweight mock-neck compression suit. He zipped it up and reached for his black riding suit, then pulled it on. The suit was made of a featherweight material reminiscent of leather, the new breed of protective racing gear that he and Grey had designed several years before. Unlike the more traditional bulky riding suits, this one hardened like an exoskeleton upon impact while releasing a cushioning system on the inside to protect the rider. The boots and gloves had similar qualities but remained flexible if the rider needed to ward off an attack.

After securing the jeweled dagger, wafers, and his firearm, he headed down to the garage to retrieve his bike, helmet, and gloves. The rest of the equipment he needed for this mission was already on his bike—a customized Suzuki Hayabusa—which operated in a special stealth mode and rendered the bike nearly silent. Specially designed projection screens also made the motorcycle difficult to see.

Jake sported a feral grin as he lowered the night-vision visor. He knew he was being followed.

This is going to be fun.

GRANT and Theo watched as their mark pulled into the garage beneath the apartment building, the door closing behind him as the taillights disappeared down the ramp. A few minutes later, lights appeared in Jacob Anders's third-floor apartment. Ten minutes after that, the garage door opened again, and a dark figure on a motorcycle exited, speeding down the street. Grant maneuvered the car away from the curb and began to follow.

JAKE rode full-out on the rural roads toward the Michelson summer estate, his speed increasing as he left the confines of the city. He loved the feel of the wind buffeting his body as he traveled down the quiet highway. With the bike in stealth mode, he flew by the tiny towns along the route. He toyed with his tail, circling around and following the black Jag before passing it for good.

Less than an hour later, he arrived at his destination: the farthest reaches of the Michelson estate, the family crypt and gardens. He parked just to the side of the entrance and got off the bike, then left his helmet and gloves atop the seat. The lock on the gate was easy to open.

He headed for the white stone building, breathing in the cool air and the sweet scent of flowers.

He knew exactly what he needed to do; the Sim had revealed it all to him. Noting the lock on the mausoleum door and smiling in admiration at the ingenuity of the device, he pulled the dagger out of his belt and slipped the blade inside like a key. The jewels in the knife's hilt glowed as he turned the handle. The door opened, and he strode confidently inside. He shined an LED flashlight onto the glass-encased wall that held the urns with the remains of members of the Michelson family long passed. For a moment, he paused by the urn that read "Trace Michelson." Then, with his face set in a determined frown, he continued on to locate Trace's grandfather's tomb.

Alfred Michelson's body, however, was not found behind the beautifully lit glass enclosure, but rested instead behind a white-and-silver marble wall. Trace hadn't cremated his grandfather's remains. Suspecting that the old man had been murdered, he had wanted to preserve the body.

Jake spotted what he'd been looking for on the wall near Alfred's sealed tomb—a gold disk attached to the marble and engraved with the date of the old man's death. He pried the disk off, then inserted the wafers into the three slots in the shallow hole behind it.

Once the wafers were inserted, a projection of the same mandala he'd seen in Nepal appeared on the wall in front of him. The highest concentration of color in the projection fell upon an urn belonging to one of Trace's cousins, Reese Michelson. The glass door, responding to the light of the mandala, clicked open.

Jake retrieved the urn. It was surprisingly light in spite of its size. He opened the top and, inside, found a microchip—the duplicate of the Sim implanted in his own body. He pulled the chip out and placed it in a small case in his jacket, then returned the urn, retrieved the wafers, and replaced the gold disk. The glass door clicked shut, sealing the remains of the Michelson clan members behind it once more.

Before turning to head out through the mausoleum door, he asked casually, "What took ya so long, Schaeffer?"

"Just wanted to see what you were doing with the property you stole from the Trust. I never took you for a necrophiliac, Anders."

Grant moved into the mausoleum and away from the door, his gun pointed at Jake.

"There's a lot you don't know 'bout me."

"Hand the stuff over, Anders."

"Or what? You'll kill me? Not likely." Grant held his gun level with Jake's chest, and Jake laughed as the other agent approached him. "Shoot me if you can, Schaeffer. Haddon doesn't want me dead. Not yet, at least."

"You're trash, Anders. Your survival isn't in the least bit important to me."

"And you're dirty, Schaeffer. You and your scumbag buddy Sandoval. Were you in on the Union Station gig too?"

"If it had been me in that bathroom, *you'd* be the corpse, not Sandoval. You're a crazy fuck. I always knew that. This just confirms it for me." The gun he held did not waver.

"Jake, he will *shoot you. And if he doesn't, his partner is waiting in the car just at the edge of the property to finish the job."*

I don't care. I can heal myself.

"You calling me paranoid? Insane?" Jake taunted as he licked his lips. "Maybe I am." He now stood within point-blank range of the other man's weapon.

"Jake, testing your healing capability is not prudent at this time," Trace warned.

Grey won't do it, so I have to find someone else to test my theory, don't I?

"Jake, what the fuck are you doing?" Grey appeared in the doorway, his gun drawn. He looked from one man to the other, clearly horrified.

"Testing my theory," Jake replied with calm resolve, never once breaking eye contact with Grant. "Shoot me or I will kill *you*, Schaeffer." He grabbed Grant's arm and pulled it until the barrel of the other man's gun touched his chest. "Here"—he smirked—"let me make it easier for you."

He squeezed Grant's hand, and the gun discharged.

Jake felt the bullet enter his chest. There was no pain this time, only a rush of adrenaline better than any thrill ride had ever provided him. He laughed, then just as quickly began to cough up blood, all the while continuing to maintain his grip on the stunned Grant, who fired off another shot.

The force of the second blast shuddered through Jake's body, but he still managed to twist Schaeffer's arm. It broke with an audible crack, and the gun fell from his now useless hand. Jake spat out the blood that had pooled in his mouth, pulled out a knife, and slit the other man's throat. Grant was dead before he hit the ground.

Jake backed up a few shaky steps and collapsed to the floor in a heap.

"Jake!" shouted Grey, rushing forward and catching him before his head hit the ground. He held his friend, his eyes full of fear. "You asshole! You *fucking* idiot! Why?"

He looked up into Grey's face and smiled weakly. "I had to test my theory."

"Don't you fucking die on me, Anders!"

Grey tapped his earpiece. "Extraction needed now!" he shouted. "Agent down!"

"Who is down, Agent Lane?"

Jake looked at Grey, shook his head, and closed his eyes.

"Agent Schaeffer."

"Where are you, Agent Lane?"

"The Michelson estate—the family cemetery."

"Is Agent Anders there?"

"No." His voice broke. "He's gone."

chapter sixteen

They're Coming to Take Me Away

If you could flick a switch and open your third eye,
You'd see that we should never be afraid to die.

—"Uprising" by Muse

JAKE opened up the throttle, put the bike in stealth mode, and headed back to his apartment. He was on such a rush—such a high—that he needed to feel his bones rattle to bring him back down to earth.

I know you're alive, Trace. I will *find you, whether you want me to or not.*

The Sim didn't answer. Jake hadn't expected it would.

Despite the residual high from the evening's events, he was both nauseous and dizzy from the blood loss. After arriving back home, he pulled a two-liter bottle of Mountain Dew from the refrigerator and downed it quickly, followed by a large carton of orange juice and a few protein bars. He kicked off his boots, stripped out of his riding suit and the compression liner. A quick once-over in the full-length mirror revealed an angry bruise on the right side of his chest—the only reminder of the ordeal. The leather and compression suits hadn't fared nearly as well—each sported large holes with burn marks around the edges from Schaeffer's bullets. He could still smell the gunpowder.

Not bad, he thought, running his fingers over the place where Grant had shot him. He guessed that his lungs had been punctured twice and that the shots had ripped through at least one major artery. The broken ribs had healed as well.

And all in less than five minutes. Sweet.

A quick shower to wash away the grime—mostly his own blood—and he slipped into bed, reveling in the feel of clean flesh and clean sheets. He closed his eyes and reached out for the Sim, allowing his mind to drift to a tranquil place.

HE SAT cross-legged in the middle of a dense forest at sunset, cool air rustling through the aspen leaves and pine needles. In the distance, he heard the call of a hawk and the rushing sound of water from a nearby stream. A small fire burned in front of him. The scent of the pine from both the fire and the surrounding trees filled his senses. He felt the presence next to him, but he didn't turn to look; he knew who was there.

"You did well, Jake," said Trace.

"I learned from the best," he replied, watching tiny flames rise up into the darkening air.

"Nice touch, reopening the old wounds for Dr. Carroll's benefit. Haddon's convinced that you're completely insane."

"For a while there, I might have agreed with him." Jake sighed. "When did you implant the nanobots?"

"They were contained in the final round of booster shots you received before Dr. Carroll implanted the Sim. They're submicroscopic. Only someone who knew what to look for, using a very sophisticated electron microscope, would be able to spot them."

Jake lay back on the soft ground, looking up to see the last vestiges of sunlight fade overhead. A few stars had begun to twinkle in the sky.

"So the whole Sim chip thing was a ruse." Jake chuckled. "The chip in my ear—it's inert, isn't it?"

"Yes," replied Trace. "The Sim technology is imprinted on the nanobots themselves. Removing the chip will gain Haddon nothing."

"You used the chip in my ear as an On/Off switch so that when I went into the simulator, I wouldn't see you when it was removed."

"I couldn't give you all the information at once, Jake. It would have been far too risky. I need Haddon to believe the technology is contained in that chip."

"I know, but it still pisses me off that you didn't trust me enough to tell me about him before you...." He took a deep breath and stretched his arms over his head.

"So where do we go from here, Trace?"

"We," Trace answered, "go nowhere."

"You said it yourself," Jake insisted, "you're part of my body now—I couldn't get rid of you if I tried."

"I meant only that you no longer need me."

"I don't exactly see it that way."

"You've surpassed my own understanding of how the nanobots function. You are no longer the student, but the master. Let them take the chip," he continued. "I'll still be here."

Jake felt the strong hand on his shoulder as a wisp of silky black hair caressed his cheek. He sighed, releasing what remained of the tension from his body. He basked in the heady touch as long, slim fingers traced the slight bow of his upper lip, and he felt Trace's breath against his skin. He opened his eyes and looked up into Trace's face and the gracefully handsome features that he'd dreamed about for so long. The hooded eyes were filled with unspoken passion.

For a moment, he said nothing, but let Trace press his lips against his own, his tongue probing, tasting, seeking entry. He felt long fingers comb his hair, and he fought his body's response.

"No!" he growled, sitting up abruptly, grabbing the other man's wrist and pulling it away from his hair.

Trace looked taken aback, even a little offended. "Is something wrong? Have I misunderstood your need?"

"No," Jake snapped. "You haven't. You always know exactly what I want. You know my body, my mind, my heart."

"I don't understand."

"No, you really don't understand, do you? I don't want to make love to the memory of a man, to a simulation. I don't care how real this seems. I don't want this."

The Sim didn't reply.

"You really don't understand." He stood up and stalked over to the fire, putting his hand over the flame to feel the heat.

"No, I don't."

"I don't want to make love to a Sim. I want to make love to the man. I want the real Trace."

"We've been through this before, Jake," the Sim said patiently. "The man you want is—"

"Alive," finished Jake. "And don't give me that 'Trace was shot through the heart' bullshit, either. You created the technology. You created the nanobots. You'd have been a fool not to implant them into yourself."

"Jake, I—"

"Shut up," Jake snapped. "If I'm no longer your student, then don't patronize me. Just tell me where you are—where the real you is, dammit!"

"It's far more complicated than—"

JAKE awoke to the sound of his cell phone.

Dr. Carroll? What does she want?

He heard pounding at his door, and the wood splintered as it gave way. Jumping out of the bed, he grabbed his gun from under his pillow.

"Stand down, Anders!" shouted Ryan Roberts, his gun pointed at Jake.

"What the fuck are you doing here?" Jake demanded.

John Carson and Greyson Lane stood behind Roberts, guns drawn.

"The director wants you back at HQ, Jake," answered an expressionless Greyson. "Drop your weapon. Now!"

"You fucking bastard. So you were bullshitting me all along, weren't you, Lane?" Jake dropped his gun and went for Greyson's neck. Roberts elbowed him in the gut, and Carson knocked him over the head, rendering him unconscious.

"Idiot," breathed Greyson. "You fucking idiot."

THIS time, Jake awoke in Synchack's research lab, strapped to a gurney. Synchack came into the room, followed by Stephanie Carroll and Charles Haddon.

"Agent Anders, Dr. Synchack is going to remove your Sim chip."

"No! Why?" Then, looking desperately to Dr. Carroll, he pleaded, "You promised you'd give the boosters at least a week to work. You said you wouldn't have to take the chip, you—"

Jake felt a needle prick. "What the hell was that?" he demanded.

"Something to help you relax, Agent Anders," Synchack said with obvious pleasure.

Dr. Carroll, on the other hand, appeared troubled. "Jake," she asked, "do you remember what you did last night?"

"Of course. I went to bed, had a conversation with Trace, and was rudely awakened by the fucking hit squad." He struggled against the gurney straps.

Dr. Carroll looked horrified. Synchack and Haddon exchanged knowing looks.

"You don't remember breaking into the lab, stealing the decryption wafers, going out to the Michelson estate, and killing agent Schaeffer?" asked Haddon.

"What the hell are you talking about? Schaeffer's dead? You're bullshitting me, right?" His words slurred as the sedative began to take effect.

"Agent Anders," came Dr. Carroll's reassuring voice, "you need help. We need to remove the Sim chip. It's for your own good."

"No!" shouted Jake, still fighting against the restraints, but with less force than before. "You can't do that! No!"

"He is too far gone, Director," said Synchack with a smug smile. "We will have to reboot him."

"Sir," Dr. Carroll interjected, "we haven't given the boosters a chance to work—"

"How many more agents are you going to let him murder before you realize that the boosters are ineffective, Doctor?" Synchack sported an expression somewhere between a grin and a sneer. Turning to Haddon, he added, "We have the duplicate chip. What harm would there be in attempting the reboot? Michelson's notes indicate that the procedure may be effective."

Haddon frowned, appearing to consider the researcher's suggestion.

"Director Haddon," Dr. Carroll said in a measured voice, "Agent Anders obviously had no awareness of his actions. You yourself read Dr. Michelson's notes—you understand that Agent Anders wasn't in his right mind when he killed Agent Schaeffer, that it was as a result of the Sim-induced psychosis Dr. Michelson described. If the reboot fails, it will likely kill him."

"What's with this 'reboot' crap? What the hell are you all talking about?" Jake protested. "I had nothing to do with—"

"Agent Anders," Haddon interrupted, "regardless of what you may or may not remember, you are responsible for eliminating one of the Trust's assets. You're a danger to yourself and to this organization. Simply put, you no longer have a choice in the matter."

Time to get the hell out of here, Jake thought as he pulled at the straps.

"Let me help you," the Sim offered.

Unless you're planning on giving me a knife, I don't see what help you—

The muscles in Jake's arms began to warm.

What are you doing?

"*Focusing the energy in your body on a specific group of muscles,*" the Sim explained.

You can do that?

"*No, but* you *can—it's another effect of the nanobots. You're capable of concentrating your strength in a particular area of your body. You can do it without me.*"

You're fucking kiddin' me, Trace. He pulled against the straps one more time, and they snapped easily.

"No!" he screamed, hopping off of the gurney and looking wildly around the room for something to use as a weapon. "I won't let you take the chip!"

Dr. Carroll, Synchack, and Haddon backed away from the now freed Jake, and the three agents from the retrieval squad rushed through the door. He fought them, managing to knock Carson down before he punched Roberts hard in the abdomen and elbowed him in the face. Greyson grabbed him from behind before he managed to throw the other man off. After nearly a minute of fighting, the three other agents threw him to the floor, at last managing to subdue him. Dr. Carroll jammed another needle into his leg, and he struggled a bit less. Seconds later, she jabbed a third needle into his leg, and he became still.

Synchack approached the gurney, and Greyson turned Jake's head forcibly so that the researcher could remove the chip from Jake's ear.

"Get away from me, you fucking bastard!" Jake shouted at Greyson. "I should've known not to trust you."

"This is for your own good, Jake," Greyson replied, his eyes narrowed.

"Like hell it is. You know what he'll do with the chip when he gets his filthy hands on it."

Greyson looked up at Haddon, who nodded back at him. He then released his hold on Jake's head and punched him in the temple. The world went black.

JAKE awoke several hours later with a ringing headache. He was tied down to a hospital bed, this time with metal restraints. He recognized the room. He was no longer in Synchack's lab—he was back in the medical facility.

My head's killing me, he thought as the room spun around him.

"That shouldn't be a problem for you," came the familiar voice of the Sim. *"You may not be able to withstand a gunshot wound to the brain, but you can heal this damage with little effort."*

Jake focused his thoughts on the place where Greyson had hit him. His vision began to clear, and the pain dissipated.

It's good to hear your voice, Trace.

"I wasn't sure you'd think so, after our last conversation."

That was personal. This is business.

No answer.

They took the chip, didn't they?

"Yes."

Shit. You're really something, ya know.

"So I'm told."

The door to the room opened, and Greyson poked his head inside. "Took you long enough to regain consciousness."

Jake looked around the room with concern.

"Don't worry. I've got the place jammed," Grey explained. "Made it look like one of Synchack's experiments gone haywire. It's safe to talk."

"You didn't have to hit me so damn hard," Jake groused. "And what's with the timing—how'd you know I was awake?"

"The Ares Sim told me."

"He… *told* you?" Jake was pretty sure Grey had lost his mind. "How would he…?"

"Seems our chips can communicate, bonehead," laughed Grey. "He also told me about the nanobots. I have them too—I've been doing a few experiments of my own. You're not the only superman here." He then fished about in his pocket, pulled a small key out, and reached for one of the restraints.

"What the hell are you doing, Lane?"

"Letting you go. Don't tell me that you intend to stay here."

"I sure as *hell* intend to stay here. You think I went to all this trouble for nothin'? Did you get the info on the backup chip to Mitchell?"

"Yeah." Grey frowned. "It's clean—I gave it to Haddon. Told him I got it from your place when we picked you up. It looks like he's considering implanting it in himself."

"You're joking."

"Synchack claims the duplicate chip is safe to implant in another person, and Haddon seems hot to get whatever information he can from the Trace Sim. He believes the chip may give him the rest of the information he needs to recreate the technology."

"Greedy bastard, isn't he?" Jake chuckled. "But he won't get anything from the chip."

"No," Grey answered, his expression serious once more. "And when he figures *that* out, you, Jake Anders, are dead meat. You need to get your ass out of here while you still can."

"No."

"No?" Grey was clearly frustrated. "Not only is that motherfucker Synchack practically salivating over the idea of the reboot, he's talking about neutralizing you too, just for good measure. Haddon gave his blessing."

"We both know that won't work."

"Yeah? But what about the two procedures together? If you're unconscious—hell, if you're *dead*—how do you know you can resist the reprogramming?"

Jake was silent.

"They're going to kill you," Grey snapped, clenching his jaw.

"They're going to stop my heart," Jake corrected. "Nothin' I can't handle."

Grey shook his head in resignation.

"Look, if I escape, it'll just make Haddon more suspicious. I can do a lot more here if Haddon thinks I'm on his side."

"Shit, Jake," he said, shaking his head, "you really love taking chances, don't you?"

Jake grinned. "Hell yeah."

"ARE we on schedule?" Haddon asked Synchack, who sat in a chair facing Haddon's desk, several days later.

"The duplicate chip has been prepared, as you requested. We will need to wait another forty-eight hours before implantation for the last round of inoculations to take effect."

"Good," Haddon said as he sipped a cup of tea. "I'll wait for the word. I'm eager to get my hands on the rest of Trace's data. My old friend John Mitchell appears to be interested in the technology, as well. I wouldn't want him to beat us to the punch."

Vasalia Synchack stood up and smiled, inclining his head and turning to leave. "I will let you know when we're ready for implantation," he said as he walked out of the office.

Less than a minute later, there was a knock on the door, and Haddon looked up, smiling at the newcomer. "Jake," he said, "it's so good to see you. We were worried about you. Please, come in."

Jake smiled and walked into the office. "Thank you, Director Haddon, sir," he said, taking a seat in front of the desk. He sat, back straight, both feet on the floor.

"I must apologize, Jake," Haddon began after a pause.

"For what, sir?"

"I haven't been entirely forthcoming with you." He took a quick sip of his tea and offered Jake an expression of sincere regret. "Several months ago, you asked me about Sandoval and the others."

"I remember, sir."

"They were under my orders when they attacked you."

"Sir?" Jake appeared confused by Haddon's admission.

"I needed to test you, Jake. I needed to know what your Sim chip could do. Do you understand? Until then, I had no idea of the vast capabilities of Trace Michelson's Sim."

"Of course, sir," Jake responded, apparently unperturbed. "I understand why you did what you did."

"It is, of course, unfortunate that several agents perished in the experiment," Haddon added. "But that's the nature of our work, isn't it?"

"It is dangerous work," Jake agreed.

"I'm glad you understand." Haddon poured a second cup of tea and offered it to Jake. "Dr. Carroll tells me that you've made tremendous progress since the reboot."

"Yes," Jake replied, taking the cup.

"Good, good. You had us quite worried there, you know."

"I'm sorry to have worried you, sir." Jake took a sip of his tea. "I feel much better now. I feel like myself again."

"Excellent." Haddon refilled his own cup. He schooled his features in an expression of polite discomfort to indicate that he was apologizing in advance for what he was going to ask. "I realize that before the procedure, you had very little control of your actions."

"I really do apologize, sir. I—"

"There is no need to apologize, Jake," Haddon reassured him. "I understand. But there's something I'd like to discuss with you."

"Sir?"

"A few weeks ago," Haddon said, "you took a little drive."

"Yes, sir," Jake answered without hesitation. "I drove to the Washington, DC, area."

"So I understand," said Haddon, smiling once more. "What did you do there?"

"I met with John Mitchell," Jake replied.

"Indeed. And what did he tell you?"

"That the Trust has been operating independently of the CIA for years. That it's a rogue agency."

"Good, good. And what else did he tell you?"

"That Alfred Michelson was murdered and that you were instrumental in his death, as well as in the death of his grandson, Trace Michelson."

"I see," Haddon said. "And do you believe this?"

"Yes. But it was necessary to maintain the integrity of the organization, sir. The Michelsons had become a liability."

"Excellent," Haddon replied, lifting his teacup once more. "Really quite excellent, indeed."

For a minute, Haddon merely continued to sip his tea but said nothing. Finally, Jake asked, "Sir?"

"Yes, Jake?"

"How can I help you?"

Haddon paused, replacing his now empty cup on the desk. "You can help me, Jake, by telling me the name of Mitchell's inside man or woman."

"Of course, sir," Jake replied, still holding his cup of tea. "His name is Greyson Lane."

chapter seventeen

Works like a Charm

Break free of limiting weaknesses and habits into an all-accomplishing expansion of your consciousness.

—Paramahansa Yogananda

HADDON shifted in his seat, struggling to keep his anger in check. "What else do you know about the Avadhuta Group and Agent Lane?"

"Lane passed the information from the jump drive I obtained in North Carolina to Mitchell," Jake replied tonelessly. "He also intends to give Mitchell one of the two chips I obtained in the Michelson family crypt."

"There were *two* chips?" Haddon was taken aback by this revelation.

"Yes," Jake answered. "There were two chips hidden there. The second chip contains data regarding Project Resurrection. Lane knew you'd become suspicious if he didn't give you something, so he sacrificed the duplicate Sim and kept the data chip."

"Interesting." Haddon refilled his teacup. "When does he intend to pass the chip to the Avadhuta Group?"

"Mitchell has a meeting with Lane at Argonne National Laboratories tomorrow," Jake replied, "during the annual SIM conference."

Haddon paused for a moment, sipped his tea, then said, "Jake, I have a job for you."

"Of course, sir."

"I want you to follow Agent Lane to the meeting with Mitchell, recover the data chip, and eliminate both of them."

"Both of them. Understood. And if there are others involved, should they be eliminated as well?"

"Eliminate anyone who interferes."

"Yes, sir."

"You may leave."

"Thank you, sir." Jake left, closing the door behind him.

Haddon sighed and frowned deeply. *How long has Lane been noncompliant?* he wondered.

JAKE wore his hair short and dark. Dressed in a navy-blue suit, white shirt, and navy tie, and with his dark sunglasses and earpiece, he looked just like one of the sea of Secret Service agents assigned to the dignitaries attending the international conference. The opening ceremonies of the conference now over, the participants went their separate ways to attend various lunch meetings. Jake watched as several large limousines whisked the Secretaries of State and Defense away in a blur of motorcycles and flashing lights.

It took Jake very little time to spot his marks drifting off from the crowd—Lane and Mitchell were headed toward a line of dark cars. A driver opened the passenger-side door, and Jake saw Grey glance briefly about, then quickly duck into the limousine. Mitchell followed several moments behind.

The line of cars exiting the conference building extended back several hundred feet as each car awaited the arrival of its passengers. Striding confidently, Jake approached the vehicle in which Mitchell and Lane sat and drew his gun with its silencer. The man and woman guarding the car had no chance to draw their own weapons. They fell almost instantly to the ground and lay in a rapidly growing pool of blood.

Jake climbed into the limo and removed the key from the ignition. A second later, he heard the privacy panel behind him slide open.

"Who are you? Where are Agents Shackleford and Benning?" demanded Lane.

Jake turned around in the seat. "Dead. Give me the chip. Now." He pointed his gun at Mitchell's head.

"What the hell?" Lane pulled out his own gun and pointed it at Jake. "Jake, stand down."

Jake did not react. "Hand over the chip, or he dies" was his icy reply. "He'll be dead before you can shoot me. And you know, Lane, that you'd better be one damn good shot, or I'll kill you too."

"I'll die either way, won't I, Agent Anders?" remarked Mitchell in a surprisingly calm voice.

Grey moved to grab Jake's gun. Jake shot him in the head, then trained the gun back on Mitchell in the blink of an eye.

"Give me the Project Resurrection information. Now," he ordered Mitchell, who was splattered with Grey's blood.

"It will gain Haddon nothing to recover the chip, Jake. He already has all the information it contains."

"I have my orders," Jake replied. "Hand over the chip or I'll shoot you and search your corpse for it."

John Mitchell held up his hands and slowly withdrew a small packet from his jacket. "Trace would not be pleased," he said with eyes full of sadness.

"You can neither please nor displease the dead." Then, without further hesitation, Jake shot him and quickly slipped out of the vehicle. He slid two small explosive devices beneath the car: one under the gas tank, the other under the engine.

As Jake walked away from the limousine, he heard the click of the chamber of a gun. Lottie Grier had approached him from behind. Without even turning his body, he shot her and continued to walk. He calmly straddled his motorcycle and, as he was leaving, depressed a small button on his gearshift. The limousine erupted into a ball of fire as he raced away.

HADDON watched the entire scene unfold from the confines of his office, having set up "eyes" in the form of Trust executives at different vantage points, with a satellite uplink to view the action.

"Cathy," he said, depressing a button on his phone.

"Yes, sir?"

"More tea, please."

Smiling, he leaned back in his chair. *It's only a matter of time*, he thought as Cathy entered his office and set down the tray, her hands, as always, shaking in his presence.

A WEEK after the hit, Jake was restless. He'd been like that ever since he'd recovered the data chip. The job had been easy, but there was something nagging at the back of his brain, something he just couldn't quite understand. Deciding that sleep wasn't in the cards—at least not yet—he drove from his downtown apartment to the Trust gym to work out.

After a grueling weight circuit, he ran the ten-mile path from the Trust to the shores of Lake Michigan and the surrounding forested areas. By the time he arrived back at the Trust, it was nearly 3:00 a.m. Satisfied, he hit the showers to wash off the sweat and grime. He squeezed the last of the water from his hair, wrapped a towel around his waist, and walked back to his locker.

"Well, well, well, if it isn't the Trust's resident superman, in the flesh," said Theo Pilkington. He pointed the gun he was holding at Jake's towel. "Nice ass."

"What do you want, Pilkington?" demanded Jake.

"You really shouldn't be so predictable, Anders, exercising alone in the middle of the night—it could get you killed."

"Do you mean to kill me, Pilkington?" Jake reached into his own locker to find his guns and knives missing.

"Move over to the showers, please." Pilkington indicated the stalls with the butt of his gun.

Jake walked slowly toward the shower area.

"I absolutely love the shower, you know." Pilkington sniggered. "Nice, neat cleanup."

"Why are you doing this?"

"Payback, Anders." Pilkington's eyes were cold. "An eye for an eye."

"Revenge? For your asshole of a best friend, Schaeffer? Or maybe that fucking traitor, Sandoval?"

"Doesn't really matter to you, does it? You're still dead. Besides, Haddon thinks you're better than me. I'm going to prove to him you were not."

"Were?"

"Yeah, 'were', as in past tense."

Jake reached the shower stall and was about to step in when he took hold of the shower curtain and pulled it over Pilkington's head, blinding him momentarily. Then he squeezed the other man's hand until all the rounds of the gun had fired off, slapped the gun out of his hand, and kicked his legs out from underneath him.

As he hit the floor, Pilkington reached out for Jake and pulled off his towel. Jake ran back to the locker room and grabbed his shorts with the sewn-in knife. Jake turned, flicked his wrist, and launched the knife at the other man. Pilkington leaned to one side, and the knife missed his head by only millimeters.

"Nice throw, Anders. Seems I missed something from your arsenal." Jake saw that Pilkington now held a different gun in his hand—his own Colt King Cobra .357. "Nice piece. This Colt'll be a welcome addition to my personal collection." He laughed again and fired off a shot, taking out a huge chunk of wall. "Sweet! Exploding-tip bullets. Lots of mess, no big pieces."

"Jake, there's a pair of Walthers behind the leftmost sink, along with extra clips," the Trace Sim said. *"There's also a set of knives and an M-16 underneath the next sink over."*

An M-16? Bit of overkill, don't ya think?

"It was all that was available at the time."

I need a distraction to make it to the sink.

"Happy to oblige." A split second later, loud music blared into the locker room.

"Hair of the Dog." Nice touch, Trace. Jake grinned as Pilkington looked around for the source of the music.

How the hell did you do that? Jake thought as he dove for the sinks. The sound of gunshots echoed around the locker room, and bits of debris rained down on him as he located the handguns and the two extra magazines. He left the knives; he had nowhere to put them. Then, tucking the clips under his arm, he slipped behind a row of lockers.

Guy still can't shoot, he thought with a chuckle.

"Nice music, Anders," Pilkington shouted over the din. "But you're still goin' down." In the mirror next to him, Jake saw Pilkington pass by the next row of lockers, his knees bent, gun at the ready.

If he gets a shot off with my Colt, it'll take the nanobots time to heal the hole. He's the worst fucking shot, and he's got my best gun that makes the biggest holes. Not a good combination.

Jake closed his eyes and counted to five, then stood up and faced Pilkington, firing both of his guns. Pilkington managed to fire a shot that clipped Jake in the right shoulder. In spite of the sting of the wound, Jake kept shooting with his left hand.

The blood spray pattern on the wall behind Pilkington was as wide as Pilkington himself. Jake approached, looking down at the wounded man. Pilkington smiled, lifting his hand off the ground and shooting Jake point-blank in the chest.

"You're one fucking piece of work, Anders." Pilkington laughed, watching Jake stagger backward against the wall. "You take out my best friend, then you fucking shoot *your* best friend." He coughed up blood and offered Jake a catlike grin. "But I got you good," he continued, watching the blood that ran down Jake's chest from the second wound. "And even if you survive the chest wound, that shoulder won't heal nice, either. I coated your cartridges with a little acid. Should keep eating away at you. Consider it my parting gift." He laughed and laughed, then became silent.

Jake got up, staggered over to the gym office, and called in on the intercom that an agent was down. Fighting dizziness and trying to focus on repairing the damage to his chest, he realized Pilkington was right—the wound wasn't healing as it should. He was losing a lot of blood. Worse than that, it hurt like hell.

Shit. Shit, shit, shit.

In his blurred vision, he saw a slim, graceful man standing in the doorway. "Son of a bitch," he said, coughing up blood and laughing. "So *now* you decide to show up? Or am I imagining this too?"

Without speaking, the man caught Jake as he collapsed, then washed his wounds with something that stung horribly and made the acid-burned flesh, muscle, and bone smell far worse.

Jake fought the urge to vomit from the smell, taking in deep gulps of air and trying to lift his head off of the floor. Then the pain subsided, and he felt the jabs of large needles in his arm and his chest.

"Leave a wound," a voice whispered in his ear.

Jake struggled to focus on the other man's face, but when his vision cleared, the man was gone. He passed out just as the extraction squad entered the room.

JAKE awoke in the infirmary, feeling as though he'd been hit by a Mack truck. His head spun, his limbs felt heavy, and his brain was foggy from the painkillers.

"Agent Anders," a gentle voice called to him. He turned his head to see Stephanie Carroll at his bedside, loading something into his IV line. "The acid nearly burned a hole right through you. Good thing you thought to rinse your wound, or I might not have been able to repair the damage."

Jake looked over to his bandaged shoulder. His chest had completely healed; no trace of the gunshot wound remained.

"You're one lucky man," Carroll added. "Agent Pilkington, however, was not as fortunate." She patted his arm and left the room. Jake smiled.

chapter eighteen

Resurrection and Death

Never has a man who has bent himself been able to make others straight.

—Mencius

JAKE awoke with a start, the image of the mandala fading as the wind carried away the tiny bits of sand. His heart pounded against his ribs, and he was covered in sweat.

The same dream again, he thought. *But what does it mean?*

He was back in his apartment after nearly a week spent at the Trust's infirmary. It had taken all of his willpower not to use the nanobots to heal his wound more quickly—he had wanted nothing more than to get back home and get back to work.

"Breathe," he said aloud, taking one deep breath, then another. He drew himself into the meditation pose Trace had taught him years before, focusing on his breath, slowing his heart rate, clearing his mind.

The room around him faded, and he saw himself back in Nepal, seated next to Bokar Donyo, staring down at the sand mandala.

"The mandala," explained the old man, "represents a combination of the enlightened mind and body of Buddha and is considered to have great power."

"But it's made of sand," he heard himself say. "I can't take it with me. How is this supposed to help me to help him?"

The old man smiled patiently. "It is true that the mandala is a fleeting thing. A strong wind blows, and it vanishes forever from existence. But it lives on in our hearts and minds, as it will live on in yours." Jake saw Bokar raise his hand and touch him gently on the forehead. "You will understand its value."

His own room now reappeared around him, and for a moment he sat completely still. Then, with renewed determination, he closed his eyes and concentrated once more on the image of the mandala, willing it forth from the recesses of his mind. Focusing only on the image, he imagined recreating it from the bits of sand that swirled about his consciousness. He heard nothing—neither the sounds of distant sirens outside his bedroom window nor the soft whir of the refrigerator in the kitchen. After nearly two hours, he opened his eyes once more. For a moment, he stared glassy-eyed at the wall in front of him. Then, as if a light had suddenly illuminated the vast darkness, his eyes widened in stunned surprise.

He intended for me to focus my meditation on that image. The mandala is the key to the Sim's hidden memories!

Jake could see it all now—Trace's past fully revealed to him through the Sim. He relived the moment years before when Trace had first seen a vision of a tall man with long red hair as he meditated in the tiny Tibetan village beside Bokar Donyo. He watched a younger version of himself through Trace's eyes on the day when his mentor had recruited him for Project Resurrection. He heard the gunshot ring out from Greyson's gun on the grounds of the Michelsons' estate. He even felt the pain of the bullet as it penetrated Trace's heart, and he heard Trina Michelson scream as Trace lay dying in her arms. He felt….

"I understand now," he whispered. "Trace."

VASALIA SYNCHACK stood, hovering about the table in the center of the lab. By any easily quantifiable measure, the day appeared the same as any other. Synchack reviewed several files on his tablet; Krista worked feverishly over a tray of instruments, ensuring that they were all in the proper order for the day's procedure; and several white-coated lab assistants studied computer screens and scoured biomedical journals for any new publications of interest. Indeed, from an outsider's perspective, it was simply a typical day. A day like any other except that, in the place of an anonymous test subject eager to earn the measly stipend provided in order to pay his or her household bills, the subject of this trial was the director of the Trust himself: Charles Haddon.

"Sir," Krista asked in her clipped, professional manner, "are you comfortable?"

"Quite," replied Haddon, seated on an examination table.

"I've reviewed your lab results," Synchack said, tapping his tablet with a stylus. "Blood levels are within normal range. The supplements and inoculations appear to have worked perfectly. I see no reason why we should not proceed with implantation."

Haddon smiled. "Get on with it, then, Vasalia. We've waited long enough."

"I myself will implant the Sim," Synchack said as he nodded to Krista, who walked over to a computer, sat down, and began to type.

Haddon waited patiently as Synchack rubbed his ear with alcohol, pulled a small syringe off the tool cart, and injected him. "This will numb the area for implantation," Synchack explained, following the injection with a deft cut made using a scalpel. A drop of blood fell from Haddon's earlobe onto a piece of gauze draped over his shoulder.

Then, using a delicate tool that looked like a cross between surgical tweezers and pliers, Haddon watched Synchack open a small container and retrieve a tiny microchip from inside. The implantation procedure took only seconds, and Synchack sealed the small incision with a drop of surgical glue.

"That is all there is to the procedure," Synchack explained, replacing the tool on the cart and removing the gauze.

Haddon closed his eyes and, for a moment, sat completely still. Something palpable had changed, although he could not yet put his finger on it.

"Charles," the voice of Trace Michelson intoned in his mind.

Trace? responded Haddon as a sensation of warmth ran from his head to his fingertips.

"Indeed," replied the Sim. *"I hadn't expected that you would risk implanting the chip in your own body."*

And why not? Haddon retorted. *Your notes indicated the procedure is safe so long as the chip hadn't been specifically programmed to another individual's brain structure.*

"Of course," acknowledged the Sim. *"How noble of you to risk the procedure on yourself first, rather than endanger any other lives."*

You are as self-important and irritating in death as you were in life, Michelson, Haddon snapped. Then he smiled. *This time, however, you are my tool and the key to the realization of my greatest ambition.*

Foreclosing any more idle conversation with the Sim, Haddon hopped down off the table. "Is the simulator ready?" he asked.

"I take it you are feeling no ill effects from the procedure?" Synchack asked.

"Of course not," Haddon replied as he headed toward the simulator.

The door to the simulator closed with a *click* as the simulation program loaded. The red exit light over the door vanished, and Charles Haddon found himself standing in the entrance of a large nondescript corporate building in downtown Chicago. Through the glass doors, he could see a busy street congested with traffic. The crowds parted for a moment, and there, on the sidewalk outside the building, stood Trace Michelson. Trace looked directly at him, then turned and began to walk away.

Haddon had started to follow after Trace when he felt someone's hand on his arm and heard a familiar voice. "It's a trap, Director Haddon."

"What are you doing here, Agent Anders?" he demanded, irritated to be interrupted.

"I'm part of this simulation."

"Interesting. I hadn't expected to see you here."

"This is a slightly modified training program from the original that Dr. Michelson devised for Greyson Lane," Jake replied. "My program contained an image of him. This version has both of us."

A sound like a shot rent the air, and Haddon ducked for cover.

"Everything in here seems real—smell, taste, feel," explained Jake, motioning Haddon toward the glass doors, "even the sound of a truck backfiring."

Haddon looked over at the truck idling in front of the building, and it backfired again.

"This is your new reality. You can smell and taste in this place. You will feel the pain of a gunshot if you are hit. The program is designed to sharpen our minds and our reflexes."

"Fascinating," marveled Haddon, astonished at the level of the technology Trace had achieved.

"Report," Jake said suddenly, tapping his earpiece.

In his own earpiece, Haddon could hear Greyson Lane's reply. "He's circling back and headed your way. He'll be within sight range in two minutes."

"This simulation is called Cat and Mouse," Jake explained, turning away from the glass doors and heading into the lobby of the building.

"We are the cats?"

"No," came the terse reply. "We are the mice. Time to go."

Jake walked quickly to the first bank of elevators at the center of the lobby, then turned sharply toward the next bank. Passing those by as well, he continued on to the back entrance of the building, yanked open the door marked "No Admittance," and raced down the stairs. Haddon followed closely behind.

"The goal of the simulation program is to retrieve a package from 225 North Columbus Drive, 33rd floor, Apartment 3313, before Trace intercepts you," Jake explained as they continued to run down the stairs. "He will use any means possible to prevent you from reaching your destination."

Haddon grunted in reply as they descended a second set of stairs to the subbasement.

"If we get separated," continued Jake, "whatever you do, don't let Michelson get the red dot of his gun sights on you. If he does, the game is over. You die."

"Can I outmaneuver the red dot?"

"It's possible. I did it once."

"How many times were you red dotted?"

"Three hundred forty-two times," Jake replied.

The two men now stood at the bottom of the stairs, facing three doors. Jake pulled open one of the doors to reveal a narrow maintenance tunnel. He started to go through the door when Haddon grabbed him.

"That will take you in the opposite direction of the goal, Anders."

"We part ways here," Jake said. "This is *your* simulation. You'll need to make it the rest of the way on your own."

Haddon frowned but said nothing.

"Before I leave, however," Jake added, his face hard, "there are two rules you must follow while the program is running. The first is that no civilians may be harmed in any way."

"And if that occurs?"

"The program will know and respond accordingly. You, sir, will suffer the consequences," Jake explained quickly. "Is that clear?"

Haddon nodded.

"The second rule is that you need to get to the destination in fifteen minutes or less once the exercise begins. If you fail to reach your destination within the allotted time, you lose—you have failed to complete your mission."

"Understood," said Haddon.

"Good luck, sir," Jake answered before turning and vanishing down the tunnel.

Haddon considered the situation for a moment. He was ten blocks away from his destination. He turned the handle on another door, which opened onto a long hallway and a set of freight elevators.

I'll go back upstairs and make my way through the streets, he thought, running down the hallway. *Michelson can't be everywhere, can he?*

Haddon stepped quickly onto the freight elevator. A large cart used for collecting garbage from the offices above took up nearly half the car. A minute later, the elevator doors opened and Haddon spotted Trace walking across the lobby, looking around. Haddon quickly retreated to the elevator and hid behind the cart. Trace walked by the open elevator door, and Haddon waited until the other man had turned and exited onto the plaza before heading for the glass doors himself.

I'll follow and overtake him, thought Haddon, wondering why, if such a simple solution to the problem existed, Anders had been caught so many times.

Haddon followed Trace for two city blocks before he noticed a shock of blond hair in the crowd nearby—Greyson Lane was attempting the same thing as he. Greyson followed Trace soundlessly into an alley, pulling his gun from beneath his jacket as he walked. Less than a minute later, Trace reappeared on the street, making his way onward toward his destination. Haddon stopped briefly to look as he passed the alley. Lane lay on the ground, dead, his neck broken, his body discarded next to the dumpster. Haddon glanced at his watch.

Ten minutes left. He hailed a nearby taxi. It would save time and keep him relatively protected. When he opened the door to the taxi, he was hit by the heavy, sickly sweet odor of air freshener liberally sprayed about the interior. He climbed inside and gave his instructions to the cabbie, still marveling at the level of sensory detail the program had achieved.

"No can do, sir," replied the man, smacking his gum loudly against his teeth. "There's construction in that area. No vehicles can approach."

"How close can you get me?"

"East Water and Columbus Drive," the cabbie replied, starting the meter.

"Fine," said Haddon, irritated at the delay. "Get me as close as you can to the address as quickly as you can. I'll give you an extra fifty if you can get me within two blocks of the address." The cabbie raised an eyebrow, nodded, and took off down the busy street.

By the time they arrived at the closest access point to the destination, Haddon had only five minutes left on the clock. He shoved a wad of bills at the driver, ran out of the car, raced up East Water, and then headed across the street to Columbus Drive. After entering the high-rise building, he looked around and found the bank of elevators that would take him to the thirty-third floor. The doors opened. He glanced down at his watch; there was only one minute left.

The doors closed slowly, but the ride up was fairly fast. He quickly got off the elevator and sprinted to the door. He knocked, and the door opened. A nondescript woman in a business suit ushered him into the foyer.

He entered the main room of the apartment and stared in silent shock. He was standing in his own office back at the Trust. Except that it didn't *look* like his office—the décor was different, more formal. He recognized the style.

What's going on here? he thought with growing anger, wondering what Synchack had done to interfere with the simulation. *Certainly this is not meant to be part of the exercise?*

"You are late, Charles," came a familiar patrician voice. It was a voice that he hadn't heard in nearly ten years.

Alfred Michelson was seated behind Haddon's own desk. Trace Michelson was seated in front of the desk, as if the two men had been conversing. Alfred looked up at Haddon and frowned.

"I am disappointed in you, Charles," sighed the old man. "You have failed in your mission." He turned to Trace and added, "Eliminate him."

Trace got up from his seat. In one swift movement, he turned to face Haddon and pulled a gun from his jacket. Haddon guessed there was a red dot on his forehead.

"I wasn't late. I arrived on time. I made it here in precisely—"

"The exercise commenced once you stepped into the chamber," interrupted Alfred. "You took nearly twenty-two minutes to arrive at the appointed location. Didn't Agent Anders explain the rules to you?"

"Yes, he did, but—"

"Charles Haddon," said Alfred as if he were speaking to a particularly dull child, "there are no second chances in this business. The mission you were assigned required you to reach the appointed area in fifteen minutes or less. Secrets are lost and good people lose their lives when one fails to consider all the details of the mission. In this business, we cannot afford to be careless. Mankind is dependent upon our work."

"You know nothing, old man," laughed Haddon, ignoring Trace's gun. "You never did. Your grandson, however, clearly had a sense of humor to arrange this elaborate little program. But he's dead now, like you. It's time to end this farce."

Alfred Michelson raised an eyebrow.

"End simulation," said Haddon, his tone cold as ice. Nothing happened. The room remained as solid as ever. "What's going on here?" he demanded.

There was silence from both Trace and Alfred. Then, after a moment, Alfred grew deathly pale and grabbed for his chest. Seconds later, he collapsed onto the desk. Haddon narrowed his eyes, and he glared openly at Trace.

"I see you remember the scene, Charles," remarked Trace. "As well you should. You killed my grandfather. You were here, in this office, when he died."

"Your grandfather died of a heart attack," Haddon replied with a dismissive wave of his hand. "I myself performed CPR on him. I tried to save him."

"No," said Trace, his voice calm and dispassionate. "You poisoned him." He gestured to an empty cup of tea on Alfred's desk. Then, quite uncharacteristically, he leaned back on the desk, glancing at the now still body of his grandfather and sighing.

"It was quite clever, really," he continued after a pause. "Then you put a hit out on me because you knew I suspected that he was murdered."

Haddon straightened in surprise to hear this, frowning at the other man.

"Did you really think I wouldn't know?" Trace's gun was still pointed at Haddon's head.

"Spare me the lecture," Haddon replied with another cold glare for Trace. "I must admit that all of this"—he gestured about the room—"is quite impressive. But in the end, this is just a simulation. And how thoughtful of you to dream it up for me—I'm flattered that you spent so much time before your untimely demise to 'teach me a lesson', as you might say.

"Still, you're both dead," he continued, "and I have the Sim technology. And of course, I wasn't the one who ended up killing you."

"No," Trace agreed. "I beat you to the punch. I decided that I would rather die at the hands of a Trust agent in whom I had faith and confidence to do the job right."

"You staged your own death?" The idea was preposterous.

"You could say that. Agent Lane shot me through the heart. I died."

"Such a waste," said Haddon, shaking his head. "And you didn't trust Anders to do it because you knew he was unbalanced."

"No, Charles. Jake was never unbalanced. He was always quite sane. The truth is that I trusted him with *more* than just my life—I trusted him with my life's work. I also trusted him to feed you false information about Project Resurrection."

At this revelation, Haddon frowned once more. "I have all the information about the project that I need now. Anders has supplied the last bit of it that you had hoped to keep hidden, and quite willingly."

"Jake has known my secrets all along, Charles. He is a very good man." A hint of a smile played on Trace's lips. "He is also a very good actor. I chose well."

"Since you're dead, perhaps you missed the part where I had Anders rebooted and neutralized. He's no longer a pawn in your game."

"No," said Trace. "Stephanie Carroll only staged the reboot. Jake never died on the table—there were two electrode feeds. She switched them to show a flatline when the time came."

Haddon was dumbfounded.

"Does it disturb you to realize that your loyal agents were perhaps not as loyal as you expected them to be?" Trace asked. "Or perhaps you thought that they would all be fooled by your wish to 'help' mankind.

"You did an excellent job keeping most of the agents *I* hired from seeing your true colors—assigning the less palatable jobs to the likes of thugs such as Pilkington, Schaeffer, and Sandoval. But there were others, such as Dr. Carroll, Lane, and my sister, who suspected that your motives were not so altruistic," he finished.

"None of that matters now," Haddon retorted. "With this technology, I can control all of the agents, even those who were loyal to *you*."

"What you fail to realize, Charles, is that the Sim chips—both Jake's and Greyson's—were a sham. A ruse. The technology you seek was never contained in the chips."

"Then how do you explain my appearance here?"

"The chip Vasalia Synchack implanted in your ear was meant to generate this program, and this program alone," Trace explained. "The technology it contains is quite simple, in fact. It cannot be used to create these 'super-agents' you dream of."

"I don't understand." Haddon shifted on his feet and continued to glare at Trace.

"No," replied Trace, "of course you don't understand. You never did have many original thoughts. The true Project Resurrection rests within the nanobots that course through their blood, as well as mine. That technology is far beyond what you could ever imagine."

"Even if that's true, it really doesn't matter. You're gone, and the technology will be mine, even if I have to dissect Anders to recover it. It will simply take a bit longer than I'd originally anticipated."

Trace's jaw grew tense, his dark eyes glittering in the light reflected from the window. "You have failed your mission," he said, his expression glacial. "You have failed the Trust. Good-bye, Charles Haddon."

Haddon just laughed.

"Do you find this amusing?" Trace asked. "Don't you remember what Jake Anders told you when you entered the simulation? This is your new reality, Charles. What happens here is real."

Before the other man could respond, Trace pulled the trigger on his gun. He had always been an excellent shot. The bullet met its mark. Charles Haddon was dead before he hit the floor.

"WHAT is going on?" shouted Synchack when he heard the gunshot. Blood splattered on the observation window to the simulation chamber.

"Don't move a millimeter, you little shit," growled Jake, the barrel of his gun pressed to the scientist's left temple, "or I'll be more than happy to blow your fucking brains all over the lab."

Krista pulled a gun from a drawer.

"Drop it, Krista," said Greyson Lane. "I really don't want to hurt you." The gun in her hand clattered to the ground.

Ryan Roberts, John Carson, Lottie Grier, and Samuel Klein now held the other lab technicians at gunpoint. Behind them, Trina took in the scene with wide-eyed surprise. She looked pale but relieved.

Sam glanced at Jake and nodded, a slight smile playing on his lips. Jake nodded back at Sam as John Mitchell entered the lab a moment later.

The door of the simulation chamber opened with a soft clicking sound. Trace Michelson stepped out over the dead body of Charles Haddon. "Well done," he said, looking around at the stunned agents and meeting Jake's gaze.

Trina began to cry.

chapter nineteen

Playing with Fire

There is no master, there is no instructor, there is no person to tell you what you must do.

—Kirshnamurti

JAKE stood outside the main entrance of the Trust's administrative building, leaning on a railing. The well-manicured grounds were replete with flowering trees and a small pond, and the breeze blew softly across the grass, ruffling the deep green blades. The idyllic setting was a far cry from the chaotic scene inside the building behind him, where John Mitchell had temporarily taken over the role of director under orders from higher-ups at the CIA.

Jake knew that the next several months would be a nightmare spent trying to untangle the Trust's records, as well as debriefing its operatives and determining which, if any, could be "redeemed." He frowned, worried about the men and women with whom he had worked for nearly ten years. He feared for Cathy Smyth and Krista Synchack above all, and what their futures would hold if Synchack's twisted handiwork could not be reversed.

He'd left the lab without a word only a few minutes before, passing Mitchell in the corridor and inclining his head toward him in greeting. There would be time to sort out the details of Haddon's death later, and time, he knew, to face Trace. Trina's reunion with her brother must come first. She needed answers more than he, as did Greyson, who had lived for years with the guilt of having killed the brother of the woman he loved.

Damn you, Trace, he thought with a mixture of anger and sadness, *for not trusting us.*

"He trusted you all," came the voice of the Sim. *"He just cared too much about you to risk your lives in bringing Haddon to justice."*

Jake ignored the Sim. He knew that he should be relieved that the ordeal was over, but he felt as hollow and empty as the Sim's words now sounded to him. It was as if he'd lost Trace all over again, only worse. Seven months spent on the trail of a dead man. Seven months of near obsession.

That's not true. You've been obsessed with Trace from the very beginning. He frowned at this thought. *So what now—now that he's really here?*

He took a deep breath and slipped off the grounds unnoticed.

A few hours and a motorcycle ride later, he was back at his apartment, sitting in his favorite chair, drinking a beer. His phone, which he'd casually tossed onto the coffee table, vibrated angrily. He looked to see the identity of the caller, then picked it up.

"Grey," he said.

"Where the *hell* did you go?" Grey demanded. He sounded exhausted. "Everybody's been looking for you. Mitchell said he thought you left."

"I went home."

"Trina was worried about you."

"About *me?*" Why would she worry about him? *He* wasn't the one who had just discovered that his long-dead brother was actually alive and well. "I'm fine," he answered dismissively. "But how is she? I'm worried as hell about her."

"She's doing fine," came the reassuring reply. "She's a lot stronger than you give her credit. She's pissed as hell at him, but she'll get over it. He's her brother. She'll forgive him."

"And you?"

"Me? Why would I need to forgive him?" Grey sounded irritated.

"Dunno," replied Jake with a chuckle. "Maybe because he let you believe that you killed him?"

"You worry too much. I'm fine too. Yeah, I'm pissed at him, but I understand why he did what he did."

"Right." Jake lined up another empty beer bottle on the coffee table. That made four so far, but who was counting?

"Listen, Jake," Grey said, and Jake could hear the strain in his voice, "I'll be by tomorrow to check on you, okay?"

"Sure," Jake replied dully. Then, realizing how pathetic he sounded, he added, "Tell Trina I'm sorry."

"Sorry about what? She's not angry with you," Grey said. "She never believed you anyhow—hell, none of us did." There was a long pause, and then Grey added, "Talk to you later."

"Yeah. Later." Jake tapped the phone and tossed it onto the floor.

He stretched back in the chair and closed his eyes.

He wasn't sure how much time had elapsed, but at some point he became aware that he was no longer alone in his apartment. He didn't reach for his weapon, however; he'd been expecting this particular visitor. "Making the rounds?" he asked without opening his eyes.

You should be happy he's alive, he told himself. *This is what you wanted.*

"Did I come at a bad time?" the familiar voice asked.

Jake was immediately struck by the way in which that voice resonated throughout the room, so different from the voice in his mind. This voice was warm, alive. *Human.*

He clenched his jaw and opened his eyes, then stood up and walked with determination over to Trace. He looked directly into Trace's eyes and, without blinking, punched him hard on the chin. Trace didn't even flinch.

"Feel better?" Trace offered Jake a wry grin.

"Yes, thank you," he replied as he calmly turned his back on the newcomer and walked over to the kitchen.

Jake pulled two more bottles of beer out of the fridge, then tossed one to Trace, who caught the bottle easily. He appeared surprised at the gesture and raised a dark eyebrow in response, as if unsure what to make of the peace offering.

"Please," Jake said as he reclaimed his chair, "have a seat."

Trace sat down on the couch, facing him. He set the beer down unopened on the coffee table and met Jake's gaze. "When did you realize that I would be in the simulation chamber today?"

Jake took a swig of his beer and leaned back in the chair. "Three days ago."

"Indeed."

"Are you surprised?"

"No," Trace admitted. "Despite what you might think of *me* at this particular moment, my opinion of *you* has never changed. I told you years ago that one day you would surpass me. You've just confirmed the truth of that statement."

"After the hit on Grey and Mitchell, I had a lot of time on my hands. I kept dreaming of the mandala. I finally decided to meditate by focusing on that image. The Sim showed me your past and told me what you had planned to do," Jake explained, "although it left out a few of the minor details."

"The mandala was the final key," Trace confirmed. "The Sim holds no more secrets."

"And what about you, Trace? What secrets are *you* still hiding?"

"A man must have *some* secrets," came the even reply. Trace then paused briefly, as if he were considering something. "I am curious, however."

"Hmm?" Jake had already guessed at the question but was silently pleased to note the discomfort on that usually implacable face. He wouldn't make this easy on Trace, he decided.

Let him squirm.

"If you knew I was alive," Trace asked, "and you knew where I was, why didn't you come looking for me?"

Jake laughed, and there was a hard edge to the sound. "You almost seem disappointed."

Trace was silent, and Jake thought he saw something akin to loneliness in the other man's irritated expression.

"I didn't try to find you," Jake explained, "because you needed to complete your mission, and I know how *damn* stubborn you are. I figured you'd been going it alone for so long, you wouldn't accept my help anyhow."

"I only wanted to keep you safe," Trace told him. This time, there was obvious pain reflected in his dark-blue eyes.

"Yeah," Jake answered with an audible sigh, "I figured you'd say that too." He took another swallow of his beer, draining the bottle, and replaced it on the table. "You know better than anyone that I was in no danger—you're the one who helped make me nearly indestructible. Still, I figured since this was your plan and your fight, I'd just make sure that everything was in place so you could do the job."

"You contacted Mitchell."

"I didn't tell him about you. I just told him and the others to meet me in the lab and that Haddon was planning to activate the duplicate chip. That, coupled with the evidence you provided about Haddon's activities, convinced Mitchell that it was time to take the bastard down."

"The fake hit on Mitchell and Grey was quite impressive," Trace said, changing the subject.

"Thanks," replied Jake, "although most of the credit goes to Lottie Grier. She and her team were able to interrupt Haddon's satellite feed just long enough for Grey and Mitchell to slip out of the limo unnoticed. Some well-placed blood capsules and a little chaos to cover our tracks, and Haddon bought it hook, line, and sinker."

"John Mitchell has always chosen his agents well. As have I."

"Grey and I told Trina."

"About me?" asked Trace.

"No. Too risky. But we warned Trina about the hit—sent her out of town to keep her away from Haddon."

Trace frowned but said nothing.

"It pisses me off, what you put her through," Jake added. "I wasn't going to do it to her again. If she thought Grey had really died...."

"I profoundly regret what I put my sister through. If there had been another way...." Trace sighed. "But I'm surprised that you aren't angrier with me."

"Why should I be?" Jake relaxed back in his chair once more and massaged his neck with one hand.

"I kept you in the dark."

"You were just carrying out the mission," Jake responded with a dismissive wave of his hand, "just like I have, hundreds of times."

"Indeed." Trace appeared to consider Jake's words. "I hadn't expected that you'd see it that way."

"I was angry at one point," Jake admitted. "Hell, you're lucky you didn't show up two months ago." He laughed softly. "I might not have been so forgiving."

"Then I'll consider myself fortunate."

The wind blew through an open window, gently rattling the blinds, and the faint smell of exhaust from the street below wafted into the apartment. "I can tell you want to ask me something, Jake," Trace ventured at last. "Please. I owe you that much."

Jake did not respond, but considered his words carefully. Then, finally, he asked, "It wasn't always the Sim in my head talking to me, was it?"

Trace looked surprised. "No," he admitted. "There were times when I was the one in your mind."

Shit, Jake thought. He said nothing, but stared at the row of beer bottles on the table.

"Are you angry to hear this?"

"No, but I have to admit it makes me feel a bit strange to know you can read my mind."

More than just strange. It felt intimate.

"I cannot pry into your mind or read your thoughts," Trace explained, perhaps sensing Jake's unease. "But when you opened your mind to the Sim, I could sense your thoughts and feelings."

"The Sims are all keyed together," Jake said with dawning comprehension. "That's how Grey was able to sense when I was awake."

"I had intended only to facilitate communication amongst the agents who possessed Sims," Trace told him. "The rapport between your Sim and mine, however, is more... advanced. I can only speculate that this is because your Sim possesses the sum total of my consciousness. Our connection is different. Deeper."

The confirmation left Jake feeling awkward and on edge. What thoughts and feelings had Trace sensed in him? He frowned and then stared blankly at the empty beer bottles once more.

What is it about this man that leaves me feeling so uncomfortable in my own skin?

"The notes? The test subjects who were euthanized?" Jake changed the subject, knowing full well that Trace could sense his turbulent thoughts even if he couldn't "hear" them at that moment.

"Fiction. There were no deaths, no side effects from the Sims."

"How did you get into the Trust unnoticed?" Jake asked. "And how did you manage to get into the simulation chamber without Synchack seeing you through the observation window?"

"I helped my grandfather build the facility, years ago." Trace, too, seemed relieved to have left the last topic of conversation behind. "I know every passageway, entrance, air duct—every hiding place imaginable and more. There is an underground system of tunnels known only to myself and my grandfather. One of the tunnels leads to the simulation chamber."

Jake chuckled. "I should have guessed," he said as he shook his head and smiled. "It just blows me away—the level of detail—all of the things that could have gone wrong. The planning... shit, Trace."

"I took those variables into account," Trace replied, and for a split second, Jake wondered if he had heard a hint of humor in the other man's voice.

"It was you, all those months ago in Union Station. You shot Sandoval. You put the tourniquet on my leg. And it was you in the showers, with Pilkington."

"Yes."

"You saved my ass. Twice." Jake snorted. "Thanks."

"My pleasure." Trace's blue eyes twinkled.

"So how did you manage to convince Haddon that you really had died? I imagine he would have wanted an autopsy, just to be sure."

"I had Stephanie Carroll promise me that in the event of my death, there would be no autopsy," Trace explained. "I told her that I didn't want the kind of instability a probe into my murder might create for the Trust. She honored my wishes. She told Haddon what he wanted to hear—that Mitchell's men had murdered me."

"Shit, Trace—that was one hell of a chance you took. You had no idea if you could survive a shot through the heart, did you?"

"It was a risk that I was more than willing to take. I needed to protect Trina." His voice did not waver, but there was a haunted quality to his words. At last, he picked up the bottle of beer, twisted off the top, and took a swallow.

"How did you manage to convince Dr. Carroll you were dead?"

"I reopened the wound, of course. Enough to make it convincing."

"And what if Carroll hadn't been the one in charge of your body? Synchack would have enjoyed carving you up!"

"It was worth the risk," Trace repeated. "In the end, Haddon was easy to fool. He believed in the value of my research—he never questioned that Mitchell would be willing to put a bullet through the heart of his former lover to protect the Sim technology from falling into the wrong hands."

"Lover?"

"Yes," confirmed Trace.

That wasn't in his memories, thought Jake. He had suspected it, of course, after having met Mitchell. Suddenly aware of just how close Trace sat to him, he walked over to the doors that opened onto the balcony of his apartment. He needed to put some space between them, and he needed to get some fresh air.

The night was cool; a soft breeze blew in from the balcony and the moon had risen nearly full in the sky. He walked outside, leaned on the railing, and closed his eyes, trying to forget that Trace still sat silently only feet away.

Why would he tell me about Mitchell? How much does he suspect about my feelings for him?

He felt vulnerable, naked. His jaw tightened, and he took a deep breath. He wanted to be alone, and yet he knew he didn't want Trace to leave.

"Jake." He felt a strong hand on his shoulder. "I'm truly sorry I put you through so much."

Jake hadn't been expecting an apology. "Thank you," he said, overwhelmed by the simple gesture.

He turned around slowly, and they stood there in silence for nearly a minute. Finally, Trace reached out and touched the edge of Jake's jaw with delicate fingers. Jake was astonished to realize that Trace's hand was shaking, ever so slightly.

He knows I'm in love with him. He was sure of it now.

"How could he not?" confirmed the Sim.

He's known all along. He could sense the truth in the memories of the Sim now—memories that he hadn't realized he possessed. He delved a bit deeper into those memories and found something there that took his breath away.

He loves me too.

"I haven't been completely honest with you," Trace said with a frown.

"No, you haven't."

"You were so young," Trace began. His voice was softer now, more tentative, and Jake realized that Trace was afraid he would push him away.

"I was only six years younger than you."

"You saw me only as the mentor you strived to surpass. I didn't want to—"

"I know," Jake interrupted. "I can feel it from the Sim. Until now, I didn't understand just how many of your secrets you were willing to share with me." Trace met his gaze. "But why?"

"Why did I put the truth of my feelings for you into the Sim chip?"

Jake nodded.

"I wanted you to know of them." Trace lowered his trembling hand. "I wasn't sure I'd succeed. If I died—*really* died—I wanted you to know the depth of my feelings for you. I hoped that it might help you to forgive me for deceiving you."

Jake's mouth parted slightly in shock. "It wasn't just Trina. You were ready to give your life for mine."

"Yes," Trace replied. "Gladly."

Jake breathed out audibly. *Shit. Shit, shit, shit.*

Trace laughed. "I heard that," he said, his eyes reflecting the moonlight.

Jake shook his head, reveling in the sound of Trace's laughter. He realized with some surprise that he'd never heard the man laugh. "Shit," he said, aloud this time. "This is going to take some getting used to."

"My heart hasn't changed, Jake," Trace confessed. "What I left with the Sim has only grown as I've watched you over the years—"

This time, his words were interrupted by Jake's lips, insistent and powerful.

"For a man of few words, both you and that damn *chip talk way too fucking much,"* he thought, knowing full well that Trace could hear him. Trace responded by combing his fingers through Jake's hair.

Jake breathed in the scent of bergamot and lime, his lips exploring the pale skin of Trace's neck, and smiled to feel the tiny shiver of reaction from his companion. Jake, who for so many years had seen his erstwhile mentor as innately powerful and entirely unafraid, felt the subtle change in the way Trace held himself as he responded to Jake's touch. He also realized how much larger he was than his former mentor, how Trace's body was far more graceful than his own.

He was right. I saw him only as a man of unsurpassable strength—I didn't see him as just a man, with flaws and weaknesses. Perhaps it had been for this reason that he'd pushed the Sim away in the end, seeking instead a fallible human touch. *Flesh and blood.*

The wind blew stronger. "I need to go," Trace said, gently but firmly pulling away from Jake.

"No." Jake took Trace's hand in his own.

"I can't promise you more than just tonight."

"I don't care," Jake lied. "You want this as much as I do, Trace. I can feel it."

I've waited so long to feel you, to touch you, he added silently.

Trace leaned in toward Jake this time; Jake closed his eyes in anticipation.

I've ached for you, Trace admitted.

Out on the balcony, they kissed. At first it was just lips, touching. Then the kiss deepened, becoming less tentative and more exploratory. Jake pressed his tongue into Trace's mouth, straining to taste the warmth there. He moved over Trace's teeth, then pushed deeper inside, sucking hungrily at Trace's tongue until Trace ground his hips into Jake's, closing the gap between them.

A sudden gust of wind caused one of the doors behind them to bang against the frame, and it brought them out of their reverie. Jake rested his forehead against Trace's and smiled. *Let's go somewhere less breezy*, he thought. *More private.*

Lead the way.

Jake grasped Trace's hand and led him off the balcony, overwhelmingly conscious of Trace's physical presence. The thought that Trace stood so close to him, flesh and blood, made him shiver with need.

Trace pushed the balcony doors closed behind them with his free hand. Then, turning back to Jake, he parted his lips in a silent sigh as he guided Jake's hand around his waist and pulled Jake's chest against his own. He reached beneath Jake's shirt, and Jake gasped to feel Trace's fingers on his bare skin.

Jake pulled off his shirt, and he saw Trace take his measure of the muscled body beneath. "So beautiful," he said aloud. "For so long, I had hoped…." He bent down and kissed the soft skin, then began to taste it with his tongue.

Jake moaned at the gentle touch, closing his eyes as Trace's lips found a pebbled nipple and laved circles around it. He reached for Trace's shirt, feeling its soft silk under his fingertips, and then slowly—very slowly—unbuttoned each tiny fastening to uncover the pale, delicate skin of Trace's neck and torso. The black shirt fluttered to the ground atop Jake's own, and Jake drew Trace against him so that their chests touched, reveling in the feel of skin upon skin.

Jake wondered how long it had been since Trace had held another human being, and his heart nearly broke for the man whose lithe body he now sought to possess. Could one night even begin to make up for the sacrifice Trace had made to keep them all safe?

"Don't think," Trace whispered, clearly reading Jake's thoughts. "This is more than enough for me." He bit gently at Jake's nipple, increasing the pressure until Jake groaned with pleasure.

"God, Trace," Jake hissed as Trace's hands began to knead at the muscles of his arms in a slow, deliberate pattern. "Where did you learn how to do that?"

"I learned many things in Nepal," said Trace as the corners of his mouth edged upward, "not all of which I thought fit to include in the Sim's programming." His long fingers rested gently on Jake's spine as he murmured, "Let me show you." He took Jake's arm and led him across the hall to Jake's bedroom, where he gently laid Jake on the bed, facedown.

Jake, curious, peered upward into Trace's eyes, but he could read nothing there. Starting at the base of Jake's head, Trace worked nimble fingers over Jake's skin, moving in circles and pressing from time to time, releasing the tension there.

Trace moved his hands down to the small of Jake's back, then reached underneath and unbuttoned Jake's jeans, slipping them off so that Jake lay naked on the bed.

Jake heard Trace's stuttered breaths as his hands found the firm globes of his buttocks, massaging them to the point of pain. Already hard in anticipation, Jake moaned and writhed beneath Trace's touch. And when Trace brushed his fingertip over his entrance, Jake gasped. His reward was Trace's teeth nipping at his ass and the tip of a slippery finger that breached him tantalizingly.

He wondered how Trace had found the lube, then realized he'd been thinking about it, wanting to tell Trace where it was. He almost laughed, but Trace slid his finger further inside and found his prostate.

"Damn!" Jake arched his body up to meet the invader in a silent plea for more.

Trace obliged, pressing inward with a second finger and reaching underneath Jake to clasp the hardness there. Trace's hands pressed and moved about his body until Jake begged, "Please. Oh, please!"

Trace's hands stilled as he stood up and shed his own clothes, joining Jake on the bed a moment later. In the dim light of the room, his eyes were dark with passion, and Jake's breath caught in his throat when he saw that beautiful face within reach.

"I dreamed of this, Jake." His voice was husky with desire. "Of the feel of your body next to mine, of the sound of your breath against my cheek."

Jake pulled Trace's lips to his, wanting to memorize the taste and feel of them, to hold them captive. The moonlight illuminated the bedroom, and with his fingers, Jake followed the light as it gently outlined Trace's lissome body.

"Let me give you what you've wanted," Jake murmured, his lips ghosting over the curve of Trace's neck as he straddled the smaller man's hips. He leaned over and licked a line from chest to abdomen, nipping and biting almost possessively—a reminder that this was real for both of them. The tiny marks left behind would quickly fade, but the memory would remain long after.

"Let me show you what I've dreamed of." He shifted further down, his hands on Trace's hips as his mouth sought the graceful erection he found there. Trace's breath stuttered as Jake's wet warmth enveloped him, and his hips began to move of their own accord, the initial gentleness giving way to the deep and hungry need of his body.

Feeling Trace respond to him reminded Jake of the powerful, indomitable man he'd first met years ago on the rough Chicago streets. The knowledge that Trace was ceding him control—that he trusted him enough to do so—was at once the sexiest thing he'd ever experienced and the most frightening.

"Don't doubt yourself," Trace said in an undertone. "You are my equal, and more. I always knew it would be you I would entrust my soul to. Take what is yours—I offer it to you. No more the master. *Never* again the master...."

The words were Jake's undoing, and he ruthlessly took Trace's erection in his mouth, licking and nipping at the crown, pressing his tongue into the tip, and tasting the essence of the other man. He swallowed Trace's cock down, pulling and sucking, his teeth scraping against the sensitive skin until he heard Trace gasp in response.

That sound, more than anything else—the sound of Trace's voice in his ears—was something he knew he would never forget. In that moment, as he brought the powerful man to the edge of ecstasy and beyond, Jake understood that he could never again rely upon the Sim to assuage the pain in his heart. The pain would endure as a reminder, and he would cling to it to remember this night.

"Jake!" the flesh and blood Trace shouted, his capitulation complete.

Jake drank in Trace's release, sucking down what he could greedily, knowing that he would never again know such pleasure. It was enough. It would *have* to be enough.

Take what I offer you now. This time, the words echoed through his mind: the ultimate surrender.

He took his hand, still wet from Trace's passion, and rubbed it on himself. With Trace's dark eyes upon his own, he pressed without preparation against Trace's entrance, knowing that this was what the other man wanted.

Trace keened, pushing his body against his lover's so that he took Jake in as deep as possible, to the sound of Jake's ragged breaths. Their bodies joined with an intensity that shook them both to the very core. And with the melding of their flesh came a melding of their minds— more intense, even, than the physical pleasure of their union.

Trace! Oh, God! Trace!

chapter twenty

Eyes are the Mirrors of the Soul

Only an arrogant man will claim to be independent of everybody else and be self-contained.

—Mahatma Gandhi

THEY lay together hours later, entangled on Jake's bed. The feeling of Trace's body, solid and alive next to his, was a needed reminder to Jake that he hadn't made love to a Sim but to a flesh and blood man. A man whom he loved deeply.

"You gave yourself the first prototype nanobots," he said, knowing that Trace couldn't sleep either.

"Yes." Trace gazed out of the window at the clear, star-filled sky.

"You intended to give the second set to your grandfather. You wanted to protect him." He felt Trace's muscles tighten, felt his breath catch for an instant. "You couldn't have saved him." He could sense the other man's pain and guilt as keenly as if it were his own.

"If I had finished the second set in time, he might not have died," Trace whispered. "I knew it was just a matter of time before Haddon tried to assassinate him."

Jake pulled Trace closer and felt the tension in Trace's body ease a bit. "Your grandfather knew the only way to protect the Trust from Haddon was to keep him close."

Trace closed his eyes and sighed audibly. "Yes."

"But you accomplished what he would have wanted, Trace," Jake insisted. "The Trust will survive."

"A phoenix from the ashes?"

"Yeah." Jake kissed Trace sweetly on his cheek and stroked the strands of hair that had fallen across it.

"And what about you?" asked Trace.

"Me?"

"Yes."

"I'm not sure," admitted Jake. "I guess I'll go back."

"As you should."

"And you? Will you take over as director again, if they ask you?"

"No." Trace's voice was firm and unwavering. "That part of my life is over, Jake."

And us? Jake wondered as he fell asleep, still holding Trace against his body. *Are you and I over, as well?*

If you need me, you will be able to find me, came the silent reply.

Six months later

JAKE sat behind the familiar desk, leaning back in the chair after having signed off on yet another report. *Damn paperwork,* he thought.

There was a beep from his desk phone. "Director Anders, sir?" came a woman's voice through the speaker.

"*Acting* Director," he quickly corrected.

"Sir, you asked me to let you know when they arrived," said his assistant. "They're at the main entrance, sir."

"Thank you, Cathy," he replied, thinking how good it was to hear her voice once more.

"Certainly, sir. I'll see to it that you're not interrupted."

Acting Director Anders. With this thought, he stood up and walked over to the window. The warm afternoon sunlight streamed in across the desk, falling upon a small bonsai cherry tree—a parting gift from Trace. He had left for parts unknown less than a day after he'd risen from the dead to finish what he'd started so many years ago. The bonsai had arrived at Jake's apartment a few days later. There had been no note.

He sighed and closed his eyes. It had been, by any account, a challenging six months. After spending nearly six weeks sorting through the Trust's files, John Mitchell had finally returned to DC, having garnered the approval of the CIA's upper management for Trina to take over her brother's work as director. The Trust would now devote its energies entirely to research in the field of biotechnology; the "executives" had been either decommissioned or transferred to the Avadhuta Group.

Jake, exhausted from the stressful events surrounding Trace's return, had jumped at the chance to resume his research. If he never was sent on another mission, he figured he would die a happy man.

For the first two months after Trace had left, Jake worked with Greyson to complete his dissertation. The writing had taken up most of his waking hours—a welcome relief from the long nights spent alone in his apartment, wondering where Trace was or if he would ever see him again. Now, looking back at those months spent at Grey's side, Jake realized how unrealistic it had been to believe that life at the Trust could ever return to normal for him. It hadn't been a surprise when he'd received a call from Mitchell asking him to come to Washington to discuss his "future" with the CIA.

They met in Mitchell's office. Jake stopped by Agent Grier's desk first to thank her again for her help in staging the hit. Mitchell appeared tired but smiled warmly, directing Jake to the same chair in which he'd sat less than six months before, when Mitchell had told him the truth about the Trust.

"It's good to see you, sir," Jake told him.

"Please call me John," Mitchell replied. "Do you know why you're here?"

"I can guess."

"I'm sorry, Jake." Mitchell appeared sad. "I know that you've enjoyed your time in the lab. I only wish I could have convinced my superiors to—"

"Please," Jake interrupted. "You don't need to apologize to me. I always knew that the government could never overlook the Sim technology and just let me be." Then, after pausing for a moment, he asked, "Grey's already signed up, hasn't he?"

"Yes. I think he's looking forward to it. We've agreed that he will continue to be based in Chicago and work on his research when he's not out on a mission."

"A year ago," Jake said, "I'd have jumped at the same arrangement. But now, I'm not sure."

"Much has changed for you, I know."

"Trina asked me to serve as acting director while she and Grey are on their honeymoon," he said. "Would you mind if I give you an answer after she returns?"

"Of course. But I must be frank with you. If you choose to decline their 'offer', I cannot ensure your independence, either. You are much too valuable a commodity for them to just let you take a job somewhere doing research."

"I understand." Jake offered the older man a halfhearted smile. "I figured as much."

"I can promise you that I, at least, will not interfere in your choice. And regardless of what my superiors say, this must be your choice."

"Thank you... John," Jake replied.

The memory faded with a knock on the door. "It's good to have you back, Director," Jake said as Trina stepped into the office, "or should I call you Dr. Lane?" She ran to him and hugged him tightly.

She grinned and said, "Trina'll do just fine, Jake. Thanks for holding down the fort."

"John." Jake offered his hand. "I was surprised to hear that you'd be accompanying Trina today."

"Trina asked me to come," Mitchell explained as he took Jake's hand and shook it, covering it with his left hand in an added gesture of friendship. Jake's smile was genuine; in the past six months, he'd truly come to admire John Mitchell. "Besides, you and I have something we need to discuss."

Trina walked behind the desk and sat down in the high-backed chair, glancing over at the bonsai tree and smiling. "You did a bit of redecorating while I was out," she said.

"I want you to have it. It belongs here, not at my apartment."

"Thanks, Jake." She offered him a warm smile.

"I'm damn glad you're back in that chair," said Jake, relieved. "If I had to sign another report…." His voice trailed off, and he grinned. "So how was the honeymoon?" he asked. "Did Lane behave himself?"

"He was a perfect gentleman." Trina blushed.

"Right," said Jake, shaking his head.

Trina took a deep breath and assumed a more businesslike demeanor. "You said you wanted to speak to me about something when I got back," she said, looking concerned. "Is everything all right?"

Jake glanced over at Mitchell for a moment, and their eyes met. "Everything's fine," he told her. "I finally finished my dissertation."

"Congratulations, *Dr.* Anders," said Trina, her eyes lighting up.

"Thanks," Jake replied with a smile. "At least now your husband won't be able to hold his PhD over my head."

"Congratulations," Mitchell said. He put his hand on Jake's shoulder and smiled. "Will there be a graduation ceremony to attend?"

Jake took a deep breath. "No graduation ceremony."

"Jake, why not?"

"I'm leaving, Trina."

"Leaving?" she repeated.

"Leaving. Leaving Chicago. Leaving the Trust."

BACK in his apartment several hours later, Jake lay on the couch, listening to Dvorak's Seventh Symphony, a seething and turbulent piece of music that suited his restless mood. He closed his eyes, his mind once more drifting to the past—this time to Trina's wedding, to the last time that he'd seen Trace.

He stood at Grey's side, the best man, gazing at the man who stood by Trina. It was hard to remember to breathe as he watched Trace in the well-tailored tux that emphasized his lean frame and quiet grace. Jake barely remembered the ceremony later, but he memorized every expression Trace had worn throughout, the way his hair fell over his shoulders, the faint dark circles under his eyes, and the sadness there, as well.

The wedding was held outdoors at the Michelson estate on the banks of Lake Michigan, in nearly the same spot where, years before, Trina had held Trace as he had "died." Jake knew this was no coincidence—Trina, strong and determined, wanted this ceremony to symbolize a new beginning for all of them. She'd long since forgiven Trace, but she'd never forget what he'd sacrificed for her.

I've missed you, Jake thought, opening his mind to Trace's.

The words didn't come close to expressing the depth of Jake's feelings. The emptiness he felt at Trace's absence was nearly overwhelming, the Sim a pale substitute for the man and a constant reminder of what Jake had lost when he'd let Trace go.

When Trina told him that Trace would be at the wedding, Jake's feelings had been deeply conflicted. He wanted nothing more than to share his life with Trace but could not see himself leaving Chicago and his work behind. He wanted to see Trace, but he knew that seeing him would only serve to intensify the pain in his heart.

You look well. Trace's expression was unemotional.

The reception following the ceremony was just as unsatisfying. Trina, perhaps guessing at the strain between the two men, seated them at different ends of the table, at her side and Grey's, respectively. When they'd spoken, it had been polite conversation that revealed nothing of their past together or their silent grief. It was later that night, back at his apartment in the early hours of the morning, that Jake solidified his plans to leave Chicago.

Some things were worth risking it all for. Some things were more than worth the sacrifice.

There was a knock on the door, and Jake got to his feet to open it. "Grey," he said, waving his best friend inside. "I figured it might be you. There's beer in the fridge if you want one."

"What are you drinking?" Grey walked over to the kitchen.

"Nothin'."

Grey raised an eyebrow but did not comment. A minute later, he sat in Jake's favorite chair, a beer in his right hand.

"So are you going to tell me what this is all about? Trina told me what happened today."

"I'm leaving."

"Like hell you are." Grey set his beer bottle down on Jake's coffee table with such force that it nearly broke.

"I'm done, Grey," said Jake. "I've had enough."

"Bullshit."

"You know damn well the CIA isn't just going to let me sit around doing research. They want both of us for what we've got floating around in our blood."

"And what's so wrong with what we were doing?" Grey demanded. "Hell, you *loved* your work."

"There's nothing wrong with it. And yeah, I did love my work. I just don't want to do this anymore. I want—" He hesitated for a split second. "—something more than this."

"It's not just the work, is it?"

"I don't know what you mean."

"This is about *him*. And don't bullshit me. I know you too well."

Jake was silent.

"Dammit, Jake," Grey continued. "You were doing just fine until the wedding."

Jake took a deep breath and leaned back against the couch. "No, I wasn't. Even before that, I knew I'd have to leave eventually. When I saw Trace at the wedding, I finally made up my mind to do it."

This time it was Grey who said nothing.

"I've changed," admitted Jake. "I need more than just the excitement of the next mission to tide me over."

Grey laughed.

"What the fuck is funny about that?"

"Nothing," Grey replied with a smirk, "except that I feel exactly the same way." This surprised Jake. "Why do you think I finally asked Trina to marry me?" Grey finished his beer in one long swallow.

"Took you long enough."

Grey smiled broadly. "Yeah. Too long. I'm lucky she stuck around. Now I just need to get used to having her as my boss, at least when I'm not chasing all over the planet for Mitchell, that is."

"The Trust is in good hands."

"Yeah," said Grey. "Old man Alfred would be pleased."

Grey walked over to the fridge and retrieved two bottles of beer, then tossed one to Jake. They sat in comfortable silence for some time.

"Do you know where he is?" Grey finally asked.

"Nah." Jake took a long pull from his bottle. "But I have an idea. After all, he left me an imprint of his brain in those nanobots."

"Wonder what it's like to watch the world from a distance for nearly six years, watch the people you care about and not be able to speak to them," Grey mused, looking down at the bottle in his hand.

"Lonely."

"Will you come back?"

"Damn straight I will," said Jake with a smirk. "Can't have little Trinas running around without Uncle Jake, can we?"

"Little Trinas?" choked Grey. "I sure as hell hope you don't know something I don't."

"Nah. But I like the idea. I just hope to hell they don't look anything like you."

Two months later

ALONE, Trace Michelson walked the beach, his feet sinking into the wet sand, making indentations that vanished with the next wave, leaving no evidence of his presence. The sun had begun to descend toward the horizon, and the sky was a soft yellowish pink. The deep turquoise water appeared almost green in the late-afternoon light. Trace inhaled the smell of the salt water carried on the breeze.

"Trace."

Trace stopped and turned, as if he'd heard something other than just the sound of the surf. Then, deciding he'd imagined it, he continued to walk down the deserted beach, his long hair blowing about his face.

"Trace."

He paused once more, frowning and turning to face the ocean, feeling the cool water on his bare feet. It seemed an eternity since he'd flown to Chicago for his sister's wedding, and ever since then, he'd imagined hearing Jake's voice echo in his mind, a distant reminder of what he'd left behind.

Chicago. It had taken every last bit of willpower not to make more than small talk with Jake at the wedding, but he knew that if he'd expressed his feelings, he would never have been able to leave again. It had been hard enough leaving Jake before. Jake too seemed to have understood, and hadn't approached him either. Trace smiled at the memory of their only night together, then turned and walked on down the beach toward the small house painted bright turquoise, hidden amongst the palm trees in the solitary cove.

"Merci, Celeste," he said, meeting the diminutive housekeeper as she headed out the front door. "Tomorrow, then?"

"I'll be back at ten," she replied, flashing him a toothy smile. "Bonsoir!"

He closed the door behind him, wiping his sandy feet on the simple mat and running his hand through his windblown hair. He walked into the kitchen and pulled a bottle of Puligny-Montrachet from the small refrigerator. He smiled. Guadeloupe was a little bit of France in the Caribbean. Between Celeste's food and the French culture, he wanted for nothing. It was paradise, really.

Paradise, indeed. You have little to complain about—good food, good wine, beautiful weather, sand, sun, and water, and a private lab for research.

"Is that enough for you, Trace?" came a familiar voice in his head.

He looked around. How many times had he reached out for Jake's consciousness through his own Sim, hoping for a response? And now he imagined hearing Jake reach out to him. But Jake was thousands of miles away; the Sims could not communicate over such great distances.

Maybe there was some truth to the phony story that the Sims cause insanity, he thought with a chuckle.

"That depends," he heard Jake say from behind him.

He turned around and, caught off guard, just stared at Jake in surprise. Jake stood, leaning casually against the kitchen table. He had a small duffel bag over his right shoulder, and he was dressed in a pair of jeans and a simple cotton shirt.

"Jake," Trace said. "Why—?"

But before he could finish his question, Jake had dropped the duffel bag on the floor, walked over to Trace, and kissed him soundly on the lips. "God, Trace." Jake's voice was full of emotion. "I've missed you more than you know."

Trace smiled and closed his eyes, feeling the silk of Jake's hair against his cheek. "How did you find me?"

"The Sim pointed me in the right direction," Jake explained. "But it took me nearly two months to figure out exactly where in the Caribbean you were. About one month into my search, I realized that I could *see* what you see, sometimes."

Trace pulled away in shock. "You… *what*?"

"If I meditated and focused my thoughts on you, sometimes I could actually *see* what you saw. It was kinda like a disjointed dream— bits and pieces, colors. I finally pinned your location down to Guadeloupe, and then it was just a matter of time and asking a lot of questions. I'm glad I speak French—it came in handy."

"Celeste," Trace said, laughing now. "You charmed it out of her, didn't you?"

Jake grinned. "It's amazing what a little sweet-talking can do. But I think even more than that, she was worried about you. She told me that she thought you would die of loneliness."

At this, Trace swallowed hard, doing his best not to show his emotion. "So how long are you here?"

"As long as you'll have me. I'm looking for a job as a research fellow. I thought that this would be the ideal place. Gotta do my postdoc work somewhere, right?"

Trace glanced at the small duffel and raised an eyebrow. "Apparently you didn't think I'd have you for long," Trace said with mock seriousness.

Jake smirked. "I like to travel light. Besides, I took the opportunity to stash away plenty of money for a new wardrobe. I don't have many beach clothes."

This time, Trace didn't fight his emotional reaction. He pulled Jake back to him. "I'm glad you came," he murmured. "I truly am. But I can't—"

"My place is here." Jake held on to Trace as he spoke. "With you."

Trace inhaled sharply at these words and held Jake tighter in his arms. "Do you understand what you're giving up?" he whispered. "You can never be a part of that world again."

Jake pushed Trace away so that Trace could see his face. "I would have been a prisoner there."

"You'll be a prisoner here too."

"No. This is my choice. I *choose* to be with you, to live this life. If I'd stayed, I'd never have been free. They'd have continued to use me for my strength. There would have been less and less time to do my research. Eventually, I'd have been nothing more than a soldier for them. It's why you left too, isn't it?"

"They'll try to find us," Trace warned.

Jake laughed. "It took me six and a half years to find you, Trace, and you *wanted* me to. And the only way I found you this time was because of the Sim. I'm not worried. You covered your tracks well."

Trace brushed his fingers over Jake's lips. Jake sighed, closing his eyes and smiling contentedly.

"Walk with me," Trace said after a moment. He took Jake's hand and led him out the front door of the small house and down the short trail that led to the beach.

THE sky over the water was now painted in vibrant shades of orange and red, tinged with pink. The sun had dipped below the horizon, and the only sound was from the waves that crashed on the sand beneath their feet. "It's beautiful." Jake squeezed Trace's hand. *Like you.*

Jake turned to look at Trace. For a moment, he just stared at his chiseled face, watching his hair blow about his shoulders in the gentle wind. More than the incredible sunset, what he saw on that face filled him with a serenity he had never felt before. Trace was smiling—a smile of pure joy and true peace.

I went to Nepal all those years ago seeking peace, explained Trace. *I had a vision of someone who would help me put right what had gone exceedingly wrong. That someone was you, Jake, although I had yet to meet you.*

"The Trust is safe," Jake said.

Yes, it is. But I was never really concerned about the Trust.

Jake searched Trace's face for an answer but found none.

"Don't you see?" Trace said aloud. "It was *you* who put me right. It's *my* heart and *my* soul that are at peace. Just as I knew they would be."

In her last incarnation, SHIRA ANTHONY was a professional opera singer, performing roles in such operas as *Tosca*, *Pagliacci*, and *La Traviata*, among others. She's given up TV for evenings spent with her laptop, and she never goes anywhere without a pile of unread M/M romance on her Kindle.

Shira is married with two children and two insane dogs, and when she's not writing, she is usually in a courtroom trying to make the world safer for children. When she's not working, she can be found aboard a 30-foot catamaran off the Carolina coast with her favorite sexy captain at the wheel.

Shira can be found on Facebook, Goodreads, or on her web site, http://www.shiraanthony.com. You can also contact her at shiraanthony@hotmail.com.

VENONA KEYES is a modern woman who believes in doing it all; if doing it all is only in her head. She amazes people that she can be wholly unorganized yet pack a perfect carry-on suitcase for a ten-day trip to Paris. She is a believer in the "just in time" theory and can be seen sprinting in airports to the gate before the plane door closes.

She has experienced love and loss at the deepest levels and is thankful for writing and daydreaming, for it kept—and still keeps—her sane. Writing also introduced her to some of the most supportive and wonderful people, for which she will always be grateful.

Venona is a voracious reader, loves her two feline boys, volunteers at an animal shelter, is an accomplished speaker, and enjoys swimming, biking, skipping, and her beloved overgrown garden.

You can find Venona Keyes on Facebook and can e-mail her at VenonaKeyes@yahoo.com.

Also from SHIRA ANTHONY

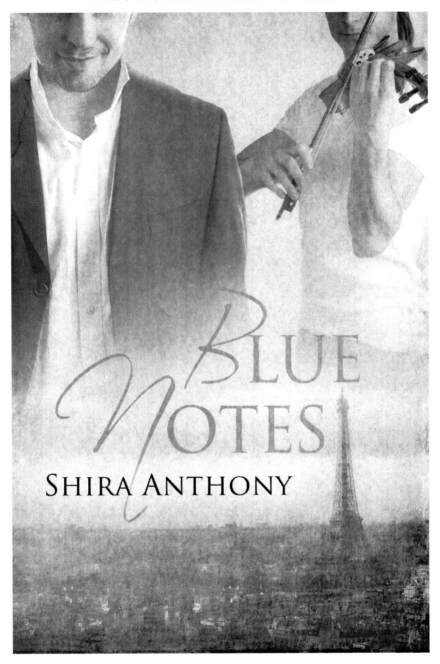

http://www.dreamspinnerpress.com

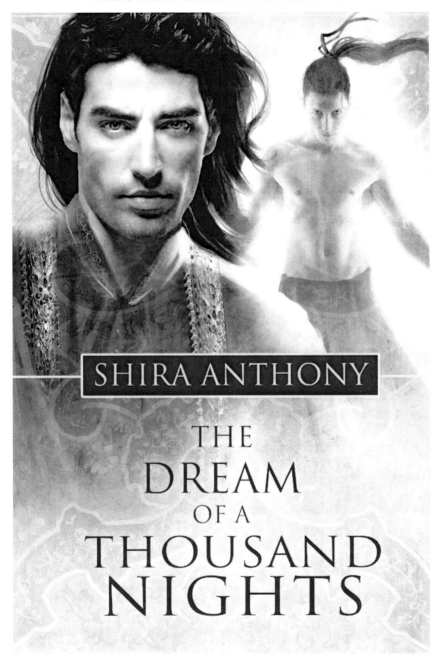

Also from DREAMSPINNER PRESS

Clare London

72 HOURS

http://www.dreamspinnerpress.com

CPSIA information can be obtained at www.ICGtesting.com
Printed in the USA
LVOW06s2127251013

358662LV00001B/13/P